SEIZED—TRIBUTE BRIDES OF THE DREXIAN WARRIORS #2

A SCI-FI ALIEN WARRIOR ROMANCE

TANA STONE

BROADMOOR BOOKS

CHAPTER ONE

"Yes, big guy. Just like that!"

Bridget leaned against the door and tried not to blush at the noises coming from within. A pair of willowy Vexlings walked past, their light-gray skin mottling as another loud moan came from behind her. She raised her glass of bubbly in salute, and gave them her most charming smile. "Nothing to see here. Nothing to see."

She took a sip of the fruity, bubbling, pink drink and felt it fizz all the way down her throat. A couple more of those and she wouldn't even notice the moaning and screaming, she thought, her fingers tingling. As the maid of honor for her new best friend's wedding, Bridget considered guarding the door while the new couple consummated their marriage to be part of her job. She knew it wasn't something listed in any bridal manual, but she didn't want a guest walking in on the happy bride and groom and getting the shock of their life. Especially not the excitable wedding planner, Serge, who was bound to come looking for the couple any second now.

Bridget looked up and down the corridor—all curved,

shiny walls, with a window arching up one side and giving a view into space—and tried to focus on the instrumental music being piped in overhead. Unless she was mistaken, it sounded like the theme song to "Three's Company." She hummed along while she rocked back on her heels and took another small sip of bubbly.

That would make sense. The space station she stood on had been nicknamed the Boat after "The Love Boat," and the aliens who'd built it—a badass warrior race known as the Drexians—seemed to have gotten all their information about Earth from sitcoms in the 70s and 80s, with a smattering of touches from more modern shows like "The Bachelor." At first, she'd thought their attempt to build a space station to appeal to earth women was bizarre, but now she found the quirky reminders of home comforting. Even if she hadn't been alive to watch sitcoms in the 70s and 80s.

"Harder!"

The scream from behind her made her jump and then glance around to see who else had heard it. Luckily for her, most of the wedding guests were already at the reception down the hall, so the wide corridor was relatively empty. A waist-high robot glided by, hovering several inches off the ground, but Bridget didn't worry about its reaction. She shifted from one foot to the other, regretting wearing high heels, even though she liked feeling taller, especially since the Drexians all had at least a foot or two on her.

After spending most of her life as a ballet dancer, her feet were a mess. Jamming her toes into pointy heels was a special kind of torture. She slipped one foot out of the glossy, nude pump and let out a sigh of relief as she placed it on the cool, white tile of the floor. She knew it would hurt even more to get it back into the shoe, but right now she didn't care. Bridget stepped out of the other shoe and emitted a groan almost as loud as the ones coming from the newlyweds.

A broad-shouldered and bronze-skinned Drexian warrior passed without glancing over, the quivering corners of his lips the only clue he'd heard both her and the loud sex taking place in the bride's dressing room. Bridget's cheeks burned, but she couldn't help watching him as he passed and admiring the view. She wondered if the Drexian warrior that had been selected for her had as nice of an ass. She hoped so. He was coming to the station from an assignment in deep space, and was expected in a few days. So far, she hadn't seen a Drexian warrior that wasn't smoking hot—all of them were huge and built—but she was impatient to see her fiancé in person.

"Seven days," Bridget whispered to herself. That was how long it had been since she'd been taken from Earth as a tribute bride. It seemed impossible that it had already been that long, but it also felt like an eternity. So much had happened in the week it almost hurt her head to think about it all.

One minute, she'd been trying to figure out how to make rent after being cut by the Miami City Ballet and the next, she was being offered money to appear on a game show. If she hadn't been so desperate for cash, she would have been suspicious of the ridiculously tall "talent scout" who'd approached her. She almost laughed as she thought back to the fake, cheesy set of "The Dating Game," where she'd met two other abducted women and accidentally discovered the game show was a sham. They were actually on a space station behind Saturn—its sole purpose to match up alien warriors with abducted human females. Bridget blew out a breath and sipped her drink. Yep, that had taken a little getting used to.

A Gatazoid walked by briskly, his short legs and spiky hair making her think of Serge again. A squeal from inside the room made the tiny man's blue hair blush pink from the roots to the tips, and he increased his speed. Getting used to the various alien species living and working on the station was one thing, wrapping her head around the concept of being kidnapped from her home so she could mate with an alien had been quite another.

She knew now she hadn't exactly been kidnapped, since the governments of Earth were well-aware the Drexians took women from the planet. It was part of the deal they'd made with the technologically superior alien warriors in exchange for protection from the violent and invasive aliens called the Kronock who had tried to invade Earth several decades earlier. Bridget had been shocked to find out that not only were aliens real—lots of different kinds, even—the governments on Earth had known about it for years.

Her first reaction, after shock, had been to tell the Drexians to take a hike. She was no one's tribute to be auctioned off. That was before she'd seen the gorgeous warriors, and learned that returning to Earth wasn't an option. Once you were selected as a tribute bride—and the Drexans only took women with few family or friends, aka no one who'd miss them—you had to remain on the Boat, either as a bride for a Drexian, or on the side of the station with the humans who'd decided not to be tributes. Since the aliens couldn't erase memories, they couldn't risk returning women to Earth for fear they'd blow the lid off the secret treaty and send the planet into chaos.

The idea of being sent to live with the women who'd rejected the offer hadn't appealed, especially when Bridget had gotten a look at the holographic environments created for the tribute brides—from blissful Polynesian overwater bungalows, to cozy mountainside chalets, to charming European villages. Her own bungalow was a luxurious chalet with a roaring fire-place, and snow falling gently out her window, along with a perfect ski slope just outside her door. A far cry from her life in Miami, but something she'd always dreamed about.

"Yes, Dorn, yes!"

"Get it, girl." Bridget murmured to herself, flicking her gaze to the door. The arrangement had worked out for her new friend, Mandy. The former Instagram influencer had been even less receptive to the idea, and now she was deliriously happy with her Drexian. She smiled, thinking about the friend she'd only known for a week. Mandy was a tribute bride like her, and although they'd become close friends in a short period of time, they couldn't have been more different. Even Mandy would admit she'd been a spoiled rich girl on Earth, while Bridget had worked herself to the bone for everything she'd ever gotten in life. She doubted they would have been friends in their former lives, but being thrust into such a strange situation gave them plenty to bond over.

Bridget drained the last drops of her drink and felt it all the way down to her aching toes, which weren't hurting so much anymore. She looked at the empty glass. These aliens sure knew how to make great cocktails.

Bridget let her eyes close. It wasn't like she had any family back on Earth. Even her so-called friends in the dance world had dropped her as quickly as the company had. The hurt was a distant ache made even more distant by the potent booze. She knew pain. Nothing could be worse than losing both her parents when she was only a child, and then the grandmother who'd stepped up to take care of her a few years after that. Bridget always told herself if she could survive the foster system, she could do anything. And she hadn't just survived it; she had thrived, excelling in community center dance classes and catching the eye of a teacher willing to mentor her, then managing to be accepted to the American School of Ballet, before earning a spot at the Miami City Ballet. All her determination had paid off, until they'd tossed her out on her ass.

Bridget straightened her shoulders. None of that mattered. She was tougher than her lithe frame would let on, and if anyone could make the most of being abducted by aliens, it was her. She'd never believed in the true love, fairytales, or soul mate crap anyway. She was a survivor, not a romantic.

"Not joining the party?" The deep voice jolted her from her thoughts, and made her eyes fly open.

Kax, Dorn's older brother and a member of the High Command, strode toward her. He shared his brother's piercing, green eyes, but wore his honey-brown hair cut close. Bridget sucked in a sharp breath. Any man looked better in a military uniform, and that went double for brawny Drexians. A sash covered with medals crossed his broad chest, and the dark pants and jacket seemed to fit him just right. She caught her eyes drifting below his waist and forced herself to meet his gaze.

"I'm . . ." she jerked a thumb behind her, "waiting for your brother and Mandy."

He cleared his throat as a roar came from inside the room. "I see. I suppose we don't want anyone walking in."

"Especially not Serge," Bridget said, grinning at Kax and feeling her arms tingle.

He laughed. "I imagine that wouldn't be fun for anyone." He glanced back at the door leading into the reception. "How about I keep Serge busy for you?"

She nodded. "That would be great. Thanks."

The corners of his eyes crinkled, as he smiled at her and turned. Bridget couldn't help feeling a flutter in her stomach. *Get a grip, girl. You're taken.*

"Taken, but not dead," she murmured as she twisted to

watch him walk away from her and disappear into the reception room.

A heavy hand clamped down on her shoulder, and she felt a sharp pain in her neck as she tried to spin around. What the hell? Before she could see who was behind her and why the vise-like grip was biting into her flesh, she heard the sound of glass shattering and everything went black.

CHAPTER TWO

Kax paused at the doorway leading into his brother's wedding reception and looked back at Bridget. Why did Mandy's maid-of-honor have to be so, well, so intriguing? Even though spitfire Mandy was the ideal match for his brother, the woman with glossy, black hair and light-brown skin had always appealed to him more.

He watched her standing against the doorway, the long, silky lavender dress hugging her curves and making him imagine the toned legs beneath it. He wasn't sure if it was her mischievous smile or the steely determination he felt from her, but he couldn't deny being drawn to Bridget.

It didn't matter, he reminded himself as he shook his head. She was promised to another.

Kax turned back to the reception and walked across the fake grass and the shiny, white dance floor to the bar. He ordered a Noovian whiskey and took a long swallow, letting the drink burn as it coursed down his throat. That was better. He'd never been one for drinking his problems away, but if you couldn't toss back a few at a wedding, when could you?

If he'd thought there were a lot of pink flowers at the ceremony, even more blanketed the reception. Chandeliers made entirely of pale-pink roses hung over the dance floor, and each long, rectangular table featured a lush runner of flowers interspersed with tall candles encased in glass. Twinkling lights were suspended in midair and the dance floor sparkled from within every time someone stepped on it.

"What do you think of the firefly effect?" Serge asked, sidling up to him. The Gatazoid reached his chest, but only because he had on a pair of his trademark platform shoes. Kax wouldn't consider himself one to notice fashion, but even he couldn't miss the fact that Serge wore a deep-rose suit, with wide-lapels in a paler shade of pink. Clearly, the wedding planner liked to coordinate with the wedding colors.

"The firefly effect?" He took another gulp of his green whiskey.

Serge fluttered a hand in the air. "They have these tiny insects on Earth that fly around and light up at night. Apparently, it's considered charming. Preston replicated the look with our technology just like he created the fake fluttering butterflies for the ceremony."

Kax nodded. "Well, I'm glad the air isn't filled with actual light-up insects."

"That makes two of us." Serge made a face and touched a hand to his spiky purple hair. "So unsanitary."

"I believe congratulations are in order," Kax said. "You managed to pull together an impressive wedding in only a few days."

"You have no idea." Serge dropped his voice to a conspiratorial whisper. "Your brother did not give me much time, and Mandy wasn't my easiest bride. At least not at first."

"I can imagine." Kax remembered his brother's tales of his difficult mate and couldn't help grinning. He knew when he'd picked Mandy for his brother that Dorn required someone to challenge him. Luckily the two hadn't killed each other before they'd realized how perfect they were together.

Serge pivoted and scanned the room. "You haven't seen the couple lately, have you? It's almost time for introductions."

Kax thought of Bridget guarding the dressing room door. "Actually, I did see them and they wanted me to tell you they're on their way. The bride is freshening up."

Serge rocked back on his chunky, pink shoes. "Excellent. I'd hate to get off schedule."

A thin Vexling with a swirl of blue hair making her almost as tall as Kax bustled up, her wide eyes blinking rapidly. "I haven't seen the bride and groom since the ceremony. Have you?"

Serge took her spindly fingers in his smaller hand and patted them. "The High Commander says they're on their way, Reina."

She sagged and gave Kax a grateful smile. "I thought I'd lost them, or they'd snuck away to their suite again. It's been impossible to keep them out of there."

Kax grinned as he watched the Vexling flush and then begin to stammer.

"It's okay," he said. "I know they haven't been the easiest couple. I'm sure they're both grateful for all your help, though."

Both Reina and Serge beamed from the compliment. Reina even sniffled and dabbed at her eyes, while Serge cleared his throat. He'd need to remind his brother to thank the wedding planner and his mate's personal liaison profusely. After surviving the pair's tumultuous courtship, the Gatazoid and Vexling deserved commendations, and perhaps a raise.

"When will I be planning your wedding, High Commander?" Serge said, then Reina sucked in her breath and Serge's hair flushed at the roots. Kax knew the little man had remembered why there would be no wedding in his future as he stammered out some gibberish. "I mean. . . Not that you. . . I apologize for. . ."

Kax pounded back his remaining Noovian whiskey, grateful as it scorched his throat, then he thumped the stammering Gatazoid on the back. "It's okay. I'm fine with it."

Serge gaped at him, his hair now fully pink, and Reina's large eyes were unblinking as Kax turned and headed across the room.

He wasn't fine with it. Not really, but what could he do? Exposure to radiation on a mission years earlier had left him unable to procreate, so his people wouldn't waste a precious tribute bride on him. Not even for a member of the elite ruling class and High Command. The rules governing how many women they could take from Earth were strict, which meant warriors waited to be matched, sometimes for years. It also meant they couldn't risk pairing a bride with a Drexian who could never produce more Drexians. Not when there had been no females of their species born in a generation.

Kax pulled himself up to his full height. There was no use dwelling on what he couldn't change. He had plenty to keep him occupied, including his return to military intelligence. There was nothing like sneaking into enemy territory to keep your mind off women. Even beautiful ones with warm, brown eyes and full, curvy lips.

Time to fetch his brother, even if he wasn't ready. He sidestepped a Drexian with a leggy blonde hanging on his arm and inhaled a cloud of perfume fitting the floral decor. The sooner he got off this space station and away from human females, the better. He stepped out of the reception room and looked down the corridor to where Bridget had been standing.

She wasn't there, but his eyes dropped to the broken glass

on the floor. There was no way she would have simply dropped her glass and walked off. His stomach clenched, and his heart began to pound as he ran down the hall.

CHAPTER THREE

Bridget rubbed her head as she sat up. Where was she? The last thing she remembered was a sharp pain in her neck. She put her fingers to the side of her throat. She couldn't feel anything, but she felt sure she'd been drugged. Why else would she feel so drowsy?

As she began to focus on her surroundings, her stomach clenched. Definitely not the Boat. She felt a sudden longing for the alien space station, which was odd, since she hadn't had any idea it—or the Drexians—had existed until about a week earlier. As cheesy as it sometimes was, Bridget would have given anything to be tossing back a cocktail at the Boat's tiki bar, instead of sitting on a strange, hard, steel bench.

She wished her head didn't feel so fuzzy. Her last memory was of being the maid of honor at Mandy and Dorn's wedding ceremony. Come to think of it, it had been right after the ceremony when everything went blank. She recalled pushing Mandy and Dorn inside Mandy's dressing room so they could get that sex-starved look out of their eyes. She'd been sipping bubbly and guarding the door, when her shoulder had been grabbed and there was a sharp pain.

She rubbed her arms, and wished she had something to throw on top of her dress. The spaghetti-strapped gown wasn't anywhere close to warm. The small room was cold, and little more than a cell—with all the charm to go along with it. Gray, metal walls surrounding a bench and a solid door. No windows. Nothing soft. No way out that she could see.

She stood and pressed her weight against the door, but it didn't budge. She hit her palm against the metal until it stung. "Hey! Let me out of here!"

No response. Either they didn't hear her, or they were ignoring her. Neither was good.

Bridget could feel a low rumbling beneath her feet. Her gut told her she was aboard some sort of ship. Were the Drexians returning her to Earth? Somehow she doubted it. Even though she hadn't met her Drexian warrior yet, she knew the Drexians valued the tribute brides above almost all else. And even if she didn't get paired off, it was well known that no woman was ever returned to Earth.

No, this wasn't the Drexians. Her mouth dried up as the engines shifted. They were slowing down, which she assumed meant they were arriving at their destination. After a minute or two, the ship shuddered to a stop, as did the hum of the engine.

Bridget edged away from the door. She'd been curious about where she was and who she was with before, but now the thought of finding out only made her shiver. She wrapped her arms around herself and backed up against the wall as she heard loud footsteps approaching.

The door slid open, and she saw the silhouette of a hulking figure in the dark hallway. The Drexians were big—tall and broad—but this figure was even taller, and she noticed him duck as he entered the room.

If she could have pressed herself into the wall she would have, as the massive creature with black armor straightened up and stared at her. Bridget was too terrified to speak. He was the Kronock fighter who'd boarded their Drexian ship during the attack on the space station. She remembered the way he'd looked at her then. It was the same way he looked at her now. Like he was sizing up a meal before devouring it.

"I am General Krav. You will come with me." Black, scaly armor covered his torso, but his thick, gray legs and clawed feet were bare. Even though her universal translator implant made it possible for her to understand him, his voice sounded guttural and choppy to her ears.

Bridget shook her head even though her voice quavered. "I don't think so. Not until you tell me why you kidnapped me off the space station, and what I'm doing here with you."

Krav didn't blink, but did tilt his elongated, hairless head at her. "You are here because you are needed to enhance the biodiversity of our species."

"Say what?" Did this guy think he'd captured a scientist, or something?

"You will add human DNA to our species, which will make it easier when we assimilate your planet." He took a step closer.

"What do you mean, I'll add DNA?" Her voice cracked.

Bridget had picked up enough information about the Kronock to know they were a species that invaded other worlds and decimated them, stripping the planets of natural resources, and enslaving or killing the population. It was this enemy the Drexians had been protecting Earth from for over thirty years. She also knew that in the passing decades, the Kronock had secretly developed their technology to rival that of the Drexians and had added artificial intelligence and robotics to their fighters. She'd seen other Kronock soldiers with computerized panels riveted into their eye sockets. This technological advancement had been a secret until the Kronock attack on the Boat only a few days earlier.

He looked her up and down, his black beady eyes flashing. "We might have superior technology to you, but we are still... organic."

Bridget had been around enough men in her life to know what that look meant. Great. It didn't take more than a second's glance at the codpiece of his armor to see he was fully equipped. She returned her eyes to his and glared at him. "Back up a second. What did you mean, you're going to assimilate my planet?"

Krav took another step closer. "Your planet has been a target for us for many years. We have been waiting and planning our invasion. Your biodiversity will be valuable to us, once we harvest your world for its resources. It is inevitable. As is your role, female."

She pulled her arms in tighter and tried to keep herself from visibly shaking. No way was she going to let these creeps lay a hand on her. Or destroy Earth. She didn't know how, but she needed to get away and tell the Drexians so they could warn Earth. As he took a step closer, she lifted one leg high and kicked out, her heel landing a direct hit to his chest.

He staggered back and let out a rough laugh. "Good. I will enjoy watching you fight me before you submit."

Bridget coiled her body to strike again; glad for the years of training that had made her muscles hard and powerful. "One thing you should know about me. I never give up."

"Neither do I." He made another move to close the distance between them and she leapt to the side, dodging his arm and swinging her leg around to land a blow on the back of his elbow.

Krav grunted and clutched his arm. She spun behind him and kicked at his back, sending him forward so he had to brace himself not to hit the wall. Bridget turned toward the open door and swallowed hard when she saw the second Kronock blocking her way, his red, robotic eye flashing at her. She was too close to land a high kick, so she pivoted and kicked low, but her foot did nothing to the alien when it made contact with his thigh. He stepped closer, and the bulk of the two aliens took up most of the room, leaving her little space to move. Her heart raced, and she was sure they could hear it. Adrenaline coursed through her, and her breath was ragged.

"Is that all you've got?" she yelled, trying to pump herself up to go at them again.

Krav turned to face her with a syringe in his hand. Not this shit again, she thought, a second before he plunged it into her neck.

CHAPTER FOUR

The pounding of Kax's boots reverberated off the floors as he made his way onto the command deck of the space station. He still wore his dress uniform from the wedding, and noticed a few raised eyebrows as he entered. He ignored them and tried to focus on the task at hand as he approached the captain, pounding his fist on his chest in salute before having one returned to him.

"What do we know?" he asked the Drexian, with streaks of silver in the temples of his dark hair.

Captain Varden crossed his arms. "Not much more than we did an hour ago. The Kronock managed to jump a small ship—probably not even as large as a fighter—next to us, then get through our shields by simulating a power outage for only a few seconds. Once they were through the shields, it seems they powered down and drifted in undetected. I don't know how, but whoever was on board managed to attach to the hull, slip onboard, capture the tribute bride, and leave within ten minutes."

"*Grek*," Kax muttered the curse under his breath. "They've been busier than we thought."

The Kronock had been engaging them in easily repulsed attempts at the outskirts of the solar system for decades. In all that time, they'd never shown new technology or strategic progress. The attack on the space station had changed that perception. The Drexians had learned the hard way that the Kronock were significantly more advanced than they'd let on, and posed an even more serious threat than imagined.

Captain Varden grunted his agreement. "We have some security footage of the actual abduction. It's clear this Kronock knew the layout of our station, and exactly where to go. I wouldn't be surprised if they had the ability to tap into our computers remotely."

He instructed a crew member to play the footage, and Kax watched on one of the wide overhead screens as the hulking Kronock appeared from a passageway and walked down one of the wide hallways of the Boat unnoticed. Kax narrowed his eyes as he studied the figure, and his stomach clenched when he recognized him. It was the fighter who'd escaped after boarding his ship during the attack. Kax tightened his fists as the Kronock on the screen walked up behind Bridget and jabbed something in her neck, making her go limp. She dropped her glass, which shattered silently on the screen. He'd then ducked down a passageway with her and vanished from the feed.

"Did he do anything else while he was onboard?" Kax asked, looking away from the frozen image on the screen. "Damage systems? Set explosives?"

"My security team has been sweeping every hall he walked. From what we can tell, he came on board, grabbed the female, and departed just as quickly. We detected his ship accelerating as he jumped out, and by then we'd determined the power outage was manufactured, so we were able to track him until he jumped again. Unfortunately, by the time we realized what had happened, we weren't able to pursue."

Kax waved a hand. "We know where he took her. We have her tracker."

The captain nodded but made no further comment. It was no secret they placed a tiny tracker in the tribute brides when they were en route to the station, along with a universal translator implant behind their ears.

"We've never had a tribute bride taken," the captain said. "What does High Command want our response to be?"

Kax had already spoken to the other members of the Drexian High Command, and knew their thoughts were the same as his. "We get her back with as little bloodshed as possible. It's clear the Kronock have more sophisticated weaponry than we've seen from them before, and we don't want to engage our fleet in all-out war. At least, not yet."

"They're counting on us coming after her," the deep voice came from the doorway as Dorn entered the room. Though Kax's brother was darker in both coloring and temperament, both men had green eyes that sparked when they were excited or angry. Dorn's eyes flashed as he strode toward the other men. "Don't you know it's a trap?"

Kax fought the urge to sigh as he studied his brother's intense face. "Of course, I know it could be a trap. You aren't the only warrior with command experience."

"We can't send in our fighters." Dorn's shoulders were bunched as he spoke. "From what I've seen, they'll be outmatched."

"Agreed," Kax said. "If this is an attempt to draw our forces, they'll be waiting for us. That's why it needs to be a stealth mission. One man. One ship. Just like they used to take her."

Dorn nodded, his mouth set in a line. "I'll do it."

Kax put a hand on his brother's shoulder and angled his head at him. "You're still recovering from your injury. Besides, you're officially on your honeymoon."

"Mandy would understand," Dorn said. "She's very upset her friend was taken. I have to get Bridget back. For her, as much as anything."

"I understand, brother, but I can't let you risk your life. You were just bonded with your mate." He leveled his gaze at him. "Your place is here, for now."

Dorn frowned, clearly not in agreement. "If I don't go, whom would you send? No one else has my experience."

Kax ran a hand through his choppy hair and let out a breath. "You forget I worked in military intelligence."

"You?" Dorn's mouth gaped. "That was years ago. You haven't been out in the field since . . ."

"Since my mission to locate and destroy the Kronock weapons transport," Kax finished the sentence for him. The brothers rarely spoke about the near-fatal mission that had exposed him to dangerous levels of radiation and changed his life forever. Not only was it a painful subject for Kax, since he was the eldest son in the family and tasked with carrying on the family name, but it had been the reason Dorn had been taken from his command post and assigned an Earth mate. It now fell to the younger brother to carry on the family's legacy, and the mantle rested uneasily on his shoulders.

Dorn shifted from one foot to the other. "Are you sure you're ready to go back? Years sitting on the High Command doesn't exactly keep you battle ready, brother, and this mission to get Bridget will take you into the belly of the beast."

"He's got my vote."

Both men swiveled their heads as Mandy, Dorn's mate, walked onto the bridge. She still wore her ivory wedding gown, with her chestnut-brown hair spilling down her shoulders in waves. The contrast with the dull-metal interior of the bridge and the dark uniforms of the crew was stark. She seemed to almost glow in the outline of the arched doorway.

"How did she get here?" Kax asked, swinging his gaze back to his brother.

Dorn's cheeks tinged the tiniest bit red. "She insisted on coming with me." He gave her a pointed look. "But promised to wait for me outside."

"You know how bad I am at following orders," she said to her new husband, slipping her hand in his as she took her place by his side. "Besides, Bridget is my friend, and I want to know what you're going to do to get her back."

The captain had stepped aside while the two brothers argued, and now turned from where he leaned over a console and raised an eyebrow at the bride on his command deck.

"I'm very aware you don't take orders." Dorn's voice was a low growl. "But I thought we'd cured you of your disobedience."

Mandy shrugged. "Guess not." She looked at Kax. "So, you're going after Bridget?"

Kax nodded, deciding to use his new sister-in-law to convince his brother of his plan. "They're expecting us to retaliate with an attack. I'm suggesting I take one of our smallest stealth vessels—a shuttle—so I can sneak aboard the ship where they're holding her and get her out unnoticed."

Mandy tapped a pink-polished nail on her chin. "Isn't that how they got her off this station?"

"Yes," Kax admitted, "but we think they did it to provoke a military response. The vessel I'll be taking won't even have serious weapons."

"That's suicide," Dorn said. "You'll be a sitting duck if they detect you."

"Sitting duck?" Kax gave him a questioning look.

Dorn cleared his throat. "An Earth phrase. Their language is quite colorful."

Mandy smiled up at him and leaned in closer.

"I promise I will not be one of these ducks. They're not going to detect me, precisely because I won't have any weapons signature," Kax said. "Before I sat on the High Command, I was known for slipping in and out of places undetected to gather information."

"You were a spy?" Mandy asked, her eyes widening.

"Why not let someone else do it?" Dorn asked, before Kax could answer Mandy. "Someone who's been in the field more recently?"

Kax hesitated before speaking. "Bridget was taken right out from under my nose. I must not have been fifty feet away from her, and I had no idea it was happening. I was the best man. I should have protected her."

"That's actually not one of the traditional best-man duties." Mandy put a hand on his arm. "You can't blame yourself. We were only a few feet away ourselves."

Kax let his gaze flit to his brother's. He knew exactly what the couple had been doing inside the dressing room, and for a moment, he enjoyed watching Dorn squirm. "Even if it wasn't my fault, it's as good a time as any for me to return to field work."

Dorn's own eyes grew big. "Field work? Since when?"

"I need to do more than sit on the High Command and give directives. Now that you're settled and our family is secure, I can return to work that challenges me."

Dorn's frown turned into a scowl. "Your missions are dangerous. You barely returned from your last one."

Kax clapped a hand on his brother's shoulder. "The perfect work for a single man."

"You don't want to be matched?" Mandy asked, looking

him up and down. "I know a lot of women who'd kill for a big, strapping guy like you."

Kax's face contorted for a moment, then he managed a smile. "A mate is not in my future, but I can help my people in other ways."

"Like serving on the High Command," Dorn said.

Kax gave an abrupt shake of his head. "I've already resigned and been reinstated with military intelligence. It's a done deal, brother. Now are you going to continue to argue with me, or help me plan my strategy to rescue your mate's best friend?"

Dorn agreed begrudgingly. "Only because my mate is insistent on helping with her wedding planning. The sooner I get that insane wedding planner, Serge, out of my life, the better."

The captain rejoined them and handed a digital tablet to Kax. He studied the screen for a moment, then frowned.

"What is it?" Mandy put a hand to her mouth. "Is it Bridget?"

"No," Kax said, looking up from the screen and nodding at the captain. "It's the Drexian warrior she was engaged to. His name is on the list of casualties from the battle on the outskirts."

"That's awful," Mandy said. "At least she never met him. She can't be heartbroken about a fiancé she never met. Not that Bridge is the kind to be heartbroken, anyway."

Dorn took the digital pad from Kax and scanned it, his brow furrowing. "I knew these men."

Mandy leaned into him and rubbed his arm.

"I want to make the Kronock pay," he said, his eyes flashing when he finally raised them.

"But not before rescuing Bridget, right?" Mandy's eyes went from her husband to Kax. "She's the first real girlfriend I've ever had."

"Of course not," Dorn told her, smoothing her hair back from her forehead. "Our priority is getting her back. If my brother says he'll do something, he'll do it."

Kax took a deep breath, his resolve hardening as he met his brother's determined gaze. "I will bring her back. I promise."

Or I won't come back, were the words he didn't speak aloud.

CHAPTER FIVE

Bridget's head felt heavy and her mouth was dry, but this time when she regained consciousness, she couldn't push herself up off the metal bench. She blinked quickly to bring the room into focus.

No longer in the small cell, she appeared to be lying on a table in a larger room. The walls were stark white, not steel, and lights shone brightly overhead, making her head hurt to look at them. She pressed her fingers against the surface she lay on—it was hard and cold, much like the bench from earlier. Had these Kronock never heard of mattresses or sheets?

Bridget rolled her head to one side, even though it pounded. A few machines sat nearby—lights blinking and motors humming—with tubes appearing to connect to her. Her eyes traced the lines leading to her arms and legs, and she jiggled her limbs and watched the thin tubes move in response.

She tried to sit up, but some sort of straps lay across her legs and her ribcage. She jerked against them, but they held fast. Stay calm, she told herself, even as a wave of panic threatened to overtake her. She closed her eyes and focused on breathing. As a dancer for most of her life, she'd learned to be aware of her body, and she knew the power of controlling her breath. The last thing she needed to do was become hysterical. She inhaled the strange, antiseptic air and blew it out through her mouth over and over until her heart rate was steady.

Keeping her eyes closed, she focused her senses on each part of her body. Wiggling her feet, she could tell there was a small tube inserted in the top of each although it wasn't painful. She used her fingertips to determine her legs were bare. Shifting against the straps, she could tell her entire body was bare. She took another long breath and tried to suppress the anger at being stripped naked and strapped to a slab. She didn't want to think about what they may have done to her while she'd been unconscious, but she didn't feel any pain or soreness.

She opened her eyes and raised her head off the table. She felt a moment of dizziness, no doubt a residual effect from whatever drug that big creep had jabbed in her neck. Again. She gazed down at her own body—her brown nipples were pebbled from the cool air, and two tubes were attached to the insides of her arms, but she saw no bruises or marks. Small favors, she guessed. She balled her hands into fists, replacing her sense of calm with a steely resolve. Enough was enough. It was time to blow this joint.

Bridget sucked in a breath and pressed herself into the table, making a gap between the straps and her skin. Luckily, they hadn't been fastened tightly and she was able to wiggle herself up a few inches. She paused to see if the machines reacted when the tubes in her feet popped out, but aside from a momentary flurry of beeps, no alarm sounded. Tiny droplets of blood dripped from where the tubes had been attached and landed on the table. She went back to work, scooting farther until the top of her body was free including her arms. She ripped the tubes out of them and then pulled her legs up and underneath the middle strap, freeing her body completely. Blood trickled from her arms, and she pressed her hands against the small wounds to stop the flow.

After a minute, she leaned one hand on the table as her head swam and she swayed in place. "You can do this," she whispered to herself.

The drug that had knocked her out was wearing off, but her body was sluggish, and the ache in the back of her head made her want to lie back down. She fought through the urge and straightened up, glad for the years she'd spent training her body to withstand intense stress and deprivation. One good thing about the often-brutal life of a ballet dancer—she was used to powering through pain.

Once the urge to puke her guts out had passed, she ran her hands over her body to double-check she hadn't been messed with. Not only was her skin unblemished, it looked like she'd been given a full-body peel. The small scars she'd accumulated over the years had faded away, and even her feet—previously gnarled from years in toe shoes—looked unmarked and smooth. She shivered as she thought of what kind of chemicals had been pumped through her veins to make such a transformation.

Now very aware of her nakedness, Bridget scanned the room for anything she could cover herself with. She wasn't a prude, but she was cold. That, and she didn't like the idea of the creepy Kronocks staring at her without clothes. Krav already looked at her like she was dinner, and that was with clothes on. She had a bad feeling about how he intended to combine her DNA with Kronock DNA, and if she was right it didn't involve test tubes.

Unfortunately, the room had nothing but hard surfaces: a

shiny, white countertop spanning the length of one side, a metal swing arm extending from the wall, and the hard bed to which she'd been strapped. She noticed cabinets beneath the counter and began opening them. The first two held nothing but what appeared to be medical supplies, but the third contained the bridesmaid dress she'd been wearing, now wadded up in a crumpled ball.

Bridget pulled it out and cursed when she saw the dress hadn't been unzipped when it had been removed from her body; it had been ripped down the side. The panties she'd been wearing were nowhere to be seen.

"So much for getting to wear this again," she mumbled to herself, managing a dark chuckle at her own joke. She slipped it over her head, despite the fact that it hung open. Some coverage was better than none, and at least the long, lavender dress covered the important parts.

Bridget held the side of the dress closed with one hand as she sidled toward the sliding door. If she wanted to escape, she'd need to leave the room. She spotted a syringe on a nearby counter and grabbed it. She may be barely clothed, but she could be armed. She pressed her hip against a large, round button, and the door swished opened. Poking her head out the door, she saw there were no guards posted, and felt both elated and irritated. They thought so little of her ability to escape they hadn't even bothered to assign one guard?

"Their mistake," she muttered under her breath. It wouldn't be the first time she'd been underestimated. Bridget felt like she'd been proving people wrong her entire life. No one had ever expected a foster kid to make it as a dancer. Some of the hyper-competitive dancers she'd competed against were worse than any alien, she reminded herself. If she could handle the ultimate mean girls, she could take on a bunch of Kronock. At least, she hoped she could.

Hurrying down the hallway, she stopped at a set of doors that looked like they were for some sort of elevator or lift, with a call button to one side and a display above it flashing symbols. She looked over her shoulder at the empty white hallway. She had no idea where she was or where she needed to go. Was she on a ship or a space station or a planet? Where would she find a vessel to escape with, and even if she did find one, how was she supposed to fly it?

Just keep moving forward, she told herself, repeating the same mantra she'd been telling herself for years. No looking back. She had to get away and warn the Drexians what the Kronock had planned for Earth. She may not have had the easiest life on Earth, but that didn't mean she wanted the planet destroyed. She thought about the grandmother who'd raised her, and her favorite dance teachers, then her mind went to the sight of the sun rising over the ocean in Miami Beach. There were plenty of good things worth saving.

Before she could press the button to the side of the doors, the display overhead beeped, and the doors began to slide open. She leapt to the side, flattening herself against the wall and holding the syringe high over her head, preparing to stab whoever emerged. She flicked her gaze to the single small weapon in her hand. If there was more than one alien, she was officially screwed.

CHAPTER

SIX

Kax scanned the black console of his stealth shuttle, and zoomed in on the illuminated star chart. According to the tracker implanted in Bridget's arm, she'd been taken to Choor Dar, one of the planets the Kronock had invaded and harvested long ago. Lying beyond Earth's solar system, it had been declared a dead world over a decade ago, its inhabitants long since eliminated and its natural resources stripped. Just as the Kronock did with every planet they invaded, he thought, his anger rising like bile in his throat.

He studied the flashing readout on his screen. It appeared the Kronock had left an outpost of some kind, although he couldn't determine if it was heavily defended or not. No battleships orbited the planet, and he got no readouts of major power signatures from the surface. At least it was something, he thought.

He leaned back and listened to the hum of the engine as it propelled him through space toward his target. If he was being honest, this location made him nervous. It didn't make sense.

Why bring a hostage to a deserted outpost if you intended to draw your enemy into a battle? Even if they didn't know the female was being monitored, they must have suspected the Drexians would track her down at some point. Kax blew out a breath. Unless they hadn't taken her to provoke a battle. Unless they had taken Bridget for another reason entirely. That worried him most of all.

He turned his attention back to the console, running his fingers over the smooth surface. If the new readings were correct, he could land on Choor Dar without much trouble. The surface emitted enough radiation—a souvenir from the violent Kronock invasion, no doubt—that he wouldn't be detected. Kronock sensors couldn't pick up cloaked Drexian vessels anyway. At least, not that he knew. Now that they'd discovered the enemy had developed jump technology, he knew it was unwise to assume anything about their capability.

Dragging a hand through his hair, Kax inhaled deeply and tried to steady his nerves. It wasn't just the startling realization that the Kronock had mastered jump technology that made him worry. The uneasy feeling he'd gotten after coming face to face with the Kronock warriors had not lessened. In fact, he'd thought of little else since encountering them during the attack.

It had been over thirty years since a Drexian had laid eyes on their enemy, and the Kronock were nothing like he'd expected. It was clear they'd been busy over the years, incorporating technology into their own physiology to make them stronger. The warriors he'd fought were more machine than creature, circuitry grafted over scales and claws. If they'd made that many changes to themselves, he wondered what else they had in store.

If he was being honest, it wasn't only the Kronock advancements making him nervous. He was acutely aware he'd been out of the field for years and, even if he'd never admit it to his brother, he felt out of practice. There was a time when a solo rescue mission wouldn't have made him break a sweat, but he found his pulse racing and his palms damp as he contemplated what he was attempting to do.

"You have to start somewhere," he said to himself.

He'd been truthful with Dorn when he'd said he intended to resume his former career in military intelligence. This mission would help get him back into the rhythm of his old job —a job he'd excelled at before he'd inherited his father's position on the High Command. Serving on the High Command had been his birthright as a member of one of the few ruling class Drexian families, and something he'd been honored to do, but if he wasn't going to be the person passing on his family's lineage, he shouldn't be the one taking the seat. He knew Dorn would send up a cry when he realized he'd have to take Kax's place, but he hoped his brother would be too distracted by his pretty new wife to complain too much.

The vastness of space and the constant danger of intelligence work was the perfect antidote to Kax's disappointment and choking sense of unfulfilled promise. It would be better to be surrounded by light years of nothingness than to be reminded daily of the things he'd never have—a mate, a family, a legacy. As glad as he was for his brother's happiness, and grateful Dorn had stepped up to take Kax's place, it made his own sense of failure even more tangible. He shook his head and tried to dismiss his self-pity.

"Focus on the mission," he muttered, letting the words pull him from his thoughts. He stared out at the immense darkness of space as he flew at supersonic speed, the autopilot steering him around asteroids and meteors as he approached the decimated Choor Dar. He hadn't wanted to use jump technology because he knew it would drain his ship, and he needed to save his power for the escape. Kax shifted command to manual, and double-checked that his stealth shielding was activated. He disabled all communications as well as sensors, so he was flying like a new cadet—only using his sight and feel for the ship to steer.

Swinging his head from one side to the other, he saw no ships flying out to meet him as he dropped into the atmosphere. He'd already determined the tracker was sending out a signal from a building on the edge of the outpost, although the signal had since stopped transmitting, so he approached from the far side. Not that they'd be able to see anything through the brown haze of the atmosphere. He dipped through a layer of murky cloud cover, and studied the colorless surface of the planet, dotted with dull, gray buildings. Cutting his engines, he glided the shuttle to the ground a few thousand meters from where he'd originally pinpointed Bridget's signal, only engaging his thrusters at the last minute so his landing would be smooth. No need to rattle his teeth out of his head if he didn't need to.

Once he'd come to a stop, Kax peered out the front of his ship. He didn't know what the planet had originally looked like, but the Kronock had left it a wasteland. He'd managed to land behind a slight rise, but as far as he could see there was no vegetation, no trees, nothing living. The air swirled with dust and the ground looked hard and cracked.

"Charming," he muttered, as he scanned the surface readings. It was hot, the air thin and unsuitable for breathing for more than a few minutes.

He flipped up the hood on his environmental suit, zipped the transparent window around his face, and grabbed the pack containing another suit, hooking it onto his back. Unlike the clunky helmets and suits they used to use, the Drexians had developed a thin, durable fabric impervious to the effects of toxic environments—it protected its wearer from extreme heat or cold, and kept a supply of oxygen flowing without the need of a glass bubble. His suit sculpted to his body like a second skin, and adapted its color to the surroundings, making it easier to remain undetected.

Kax tapped his wrist control and engaged the oxygen, while he also checked his directional guidance system. It shouldn't take him long to reach the building, he thought, as he opened the shuttle door and stepped outside. He touched the blaster on his belt out of habit, as he closed the ship and touched his wrist controller to lock it down.

The wind felt even stronger than it had looked, and he leaned into it as he walked, feeling it buffet his arms and legs. He crested the rise hiding his ship, and dropped down on his haunches as he surveyed the surface. In the distance, he spotted the cluster of buildings making up the outpost, but detected no movement outside. No reason to be outside if you could help it.

He resumed his approach, taking up an easy jog and pulling out his blaster as he got closer. Searching the perimeter for cameras, or rooftop sentries, he saw none. Odd. It seemed unlikely the enemy would have an unguarded outpost.

"Unless it's a trap," Kax mumbled. He only hoped they'd be looking for a major incursion and wouldn't be anticipating a one-man mission.

The building from where Bridget's sensor had originally transmitted lay directly ahead, and Kax headed for the door in the back that seemed to be the least used. He guessed the Kronock had located and removed Bridget's tracker. Hopefully, they hadn't moved her. Reaching the door, he swore under his breath when he realized it had no handle on the outside. So much for not leaving a trace, he thought, as he removed a handheld laser cutter from his belt and began slicing through the metal of the door lock. It made little sound, but he knew the burning smell would be a tip-off for anyone nearby.

When he'd sliced through the bolting mechanism, he wrenched the door open, stepping inside the building and bracing himself for an onslaught of Kronock. Nothing.

His stomach tightened as he glanced at his wrist and followed the red dot indicating Bridget's last signal. Unlike the outside of the drab building, the inside was bright white with sleek walls and glaring overhead lights. He glanced down at the arm of his suit, which was changing color from the brown of the dirt outside, to the white of the inside walls. He crept down the hall and looked through the windows inset in the interior doors. The first room was a large lab, with machines whirring and blinking, and counters lined with racks of test tubes. Two smaller rooms sat across from it, sterile versions of medical bays, with the prone bodies of Kronock fighters lying immobile on metal platforms. Another room farther along held a wall of computers and a standing console with a single Kronock behind it. Kax hurried past the doorway without being spotted.

He raised his blaster as he proceeded further. Another laboratory held high tables, with other species of aliens, clearly dead and being studied. He recognized the body of a Vexling and a Noovian, both being examined by a Kronock wearing protective gear. Were they performing experiments or autopsies? Either way, why was Bridget here? He wondered if she'd been injured in the abduction, and felt a rush of anger at the thought. He passed the room without being seen, and continued creeping down the hall.

Another glance at his wrist told him to turn left, and he almost ran over a Kronock fighter. It took him less time to react than the startled fighter, and he jammed his blaster into the waist-level gap in the enemy's armor and fired. The Kronock collapsed to the floor with a crash, which seemed to echo off the walls of the corridor.

He needed to hurry. If they didn't know he was there already, they would soon. He ran to the end of the hall and pressed his palm against a large button next to a set of doors. They slid open, and he stepped into an empty compartment, letting the doors close before staring at the symbols on the control panel. His Kronock was rusty but after looking at the red dot on his wrist monitor, he located the word for 'lower level' and pressed the button.

When the doors opened, he saw another empty hallway, although his wrist told him Bridget was nearby. She must be in one of the rooms, he thought, as he spied a pair of doors a few feet away. He stepped toward them, but felt something crash into his shoulder.

"*Grek*!" Spinning around, he pulled something dangling from the impenetrable fabric of his suit and tossed it to the floor. He raised his blaster to shoot, but stopped when he saw that the creature lunging for him wasn't a Kronock warrior.

It was Bridget, still wearing the dress she'd had on at the wedding, although it now hung onto her by one tiny shoulder strap. He felt overcome with relief at the sight of her, until she threw a kick forceful enough to make him stagger back against the wall, his ears ringing.

"That's for stripping me naked, you pervert," she said, as she cocked her fist back to hit him again.

CHAPTER SEVEN

Bridget knew the Kronock came in different versions, and the huge creature in the white suit was no doubt one of the scientist creeps who'd strapped her down and taken her clothes. She'd been dismayed when the needle had done no more than prick it, but had felt a surge of satisfaction as it recoiled from her punch and hit the wall, giving a quick shake of its head. The creature may have been significantly bigger than her, but it felt good to land a blow. She was about to hit him again when he held up his hands and said her name.

"Bridget, stop." The voice was muffled behind the mask. "It's me, Kax. Dorn's brother."

Bridget dropped her fist. "Kax?" She peered through the transparent window in his hood and recognized his honey-brown hair and green eyes. "Is that really you?"

He unzipped the hood and let it fall back from his face. "It's me. I'm here to get you out of this place."

Bridget's shoulders fell, and all the fight drained out of her, although she couldn't deny the hitch in her breath as she met his eyes. Damn, he was hot, even when he wasn't in the sexy uniform she'd seen him in on the Drexian station. "Good. I wasn't sure how I was going to steal a space ship and fly off this thing. Where am I anyway? A space station? A battleship?"

Kax shook his head. "You're on a planet the Kronock decimated years ago, and it looks like they repurposed a research facility on the ruins. It doesn't seem to be heavily populated."

"That makes sense. I was hooked up to machines when I came to the second time."

Kax pressed his lips together, and took in the ripped dress barely hanging on one shoulder, looking away just as quickly. "Are you okay? Did they do anything to you?"

Although she felt okay, Bridget didn't know what they'd possibly done to her, but she wasn't about to delve into that now. "I'm fine. Just get me away from here."

Kax kept his eyes averted as he pulled out a tight roll of fabric from the pack on his back. "You'll need this once we get outside."

She held up the suit—an exact match to the one he wore and almost as big. The Drexians didn't have much need for petite sizes, she thought, as she stepped into the baggy jumpsuit and pulled the torn dress off once she'd zipped the suit up halfway. She saw Kax's eyes widen. Years as a dancer had wiped out any shred of modesty she'd once had. It was impossible to be shy about your body when you had to do quick costume changes backstage, in front of male dancers. And even though she was a bit curvier than most ballerinas, she'd always been proud of her body.

"Sorry," she said. "I didn't mean to shock you."

He looked up when she had the suit on, but didn't say anything. He snapped a metal band to her wrist, and the suit shrunk to fit her.

She patted his arm. “Don’t worry. I won’t tell my fiancé you got a peek.”

Kax cleared his throat, pulling his arm away from her. “Follow me.”

Bridget tried not to feel stung. She was used to men reacting to her, of being able to make them respond with a flick of her hair or a touch to their leg. It was second nature to her, and even if she wasn’t interested, the men always were. Except this one, obviously.

She tried to remember what she knew of him aside from the fact that he was Dorn’s brother. She knew he was a big shot, which made her wonder why he was here rescuing her. It seemed like more of a thing for someone like Dorn, or one of the other Drexian warriors from his Inferno Force—rough around the edges, and tough as nails, with unkempt hair and tattoos. Not that Kax wasn’t big and brawny. He was those things and more, but he was clearly all business, with his close-cropped hair and unmarked skin. The only change she noticed was the stubble on his face that hadn’t been there at his brother’s wedding.

They stepped back into the elevator and rode in silence. Kax flipped his hood up, and motioned for Bridget to do the same. When the doors slid open again, the scene was much different.

A pair of Kronock fighters with scaled armor and red, flashing eyes stood in front of them, and another few were approaching from the far end of the corridor. Kax fired at one of the fighters, but the blaster hit the metal armor and only knocked him back a few feet. The other fighter lunged for Bridget, but she kicked her leg high and caught him under the chin, sending him stumbling.

Kax fired at the flailing fighter, and this time, the blaster fire hit him in the stomach and the creature fell. Kax grabbed Bridget by the wrist and ran, holding the blaster over his shoulder and shooting behind him.

Bridget heard the pounding of footsteps closing in on them but concentrated on running as fast as she could. They rounded a corner, and were met by more Kronock. Kax dropped his hold on her wrist, pulled a curved blade from his waistband, and began slashing at their midsections, while still firing with his blaster. Enemy fire seared his shoulder, but he kept shooting as he pushed Bridget behind him.

She smelled burning wires and scorched flesh, hearing shrieks as another Kronock dropped. Sirens wailed, and lights began flashing, making the hallways glow red as more fighters advanced on them. Bridget noticed her suit changing color from white to red, but didn't have time to dwell on it.

"Where's the backup?" she screamed.

"There is no backup," Kax said, as he fired at another Kronock. "At least nothing that can arrive quickly."

"What? Are you crazy?" She ducked as a blast went over her head.

"We didn't want to attract attention with a full-out assault," Kax said, panting as he dodged blows and blaster fire.

Her ears rang with the sound of the sirens. "Good plan."

He dropped low and fired up into the neck of the closest Kronock warrior, and the alien collapsed at his feet. "Glad you approve." He grabbed her hand again. "Mind if we discuss this on the ship?"

They ran down another hallway, and she saw an exterior door hanging open, and beyond that, brown scraggly terrain. She was already running hard to keep up with Kax's long strides, but she pushed herself even harder as they closed in on the door.

"Release her." The voice behind her made her falter and nearly trip. Kax tightened his grip on her hand and pulled her up, his face grim.

He must have recognized the voice, too. Bridget spared a glance over her shoulder as they reached the exit. The black-armored Kronock was advancing on them, his huge fists balled and his eyes burning with fury. Her mouth went dry as her gaze met his, and she stopped moving. Unlike the other Kronock who were fighting with precision but no passion, this one clearly took it personally.

"Let her go, and I will kill you quickly." His voice echoed off the walls, and seemed to reverberate in her bones.

Kax didn't slow down to respond, but pushed her through the door and fired behind him, missing the huge alien but making him pause.

"Don't look back," he told her, as they ran out of the building and across the hard-packed dirt.

Her lungs burned as she tried to keep up with his pace as they ran, but she gritted her teeth and pushed herself, matching each of Kax's long strides with two of her own. When she saw a ship materialize in the distance, Bridget felt like crying with relief.

Kax jabbed at something on his wrist, and a hatch on the gunmetal-gray side of the ship slid open. They dove for it, Kax closing it once they were inside and firing up the engines with another poke at his wrist. The ship rose from the ground and hovered for only a moment, long enough for Bridget to see a fleet of ships lifting off from somewhere beyond the medical building and swiveling toward them. Below them, the dark Kronock warrior stepped out of the building and looked up, his long jaw clenched in obvious fury.

"Strap in," Kax yelled, pulling off his hood and throwing himself into one of the pilot's seats.

Bridget did the same, her hands shaking as she pulled the seat's straps over her shoulders. She felt herself jerked backward as they shot away from the surface.

Kax's fingers flew across the console. "They won't be able to track us once we jump."

Bridget nodded, but didn't say anything. The ship was already going so fast she felt like throwing up.

Kax pushed forward on a throttle, and the ship shook violently, before lurching forward and catapulting them through the atmosphere.

As soon as they'd broken through the brown haze covering the planet, she gasped. Dozens of ships began appearing around them—popping into existence as if by magic.

"*Grek*!" Kax yelled, and she assumed he was cursing in Drexian. She also assumed the ships were not friendly.

Kax punched something on the console and the ship shot forward again, forcing her head back and making it hard to move.

"Shit!" Bridget clutched the arms of her seat as the ship spun. Lights blurred around them, as if they were passing through a tunnel. A very bumpy tunnel.

When the ship finally slowed, she let out a breath. "That wasn't so bad."

Kax didn't reply as he pressed several buttons on the console, and then shook his head. "This isn't right."

Bridget noticed flashing red lights on the screen in front of him. "What isn't right?"

He turned his head to her, his expression serious. "The Kronock hit us as we were jumping. Not only did it damage one of our engines, it affected our trajectory."

"What does that mean?"

"It means we're in a crippled ship, still far away from the

Boat or Drexian territory, and we're very much in the heart of Kronock space."

Double shit. That wasn't good.

CHAPTER EIGHT

Kax focused on the console as he rerouted power from the damaged engine, and the engine failure alarm stopped wailing. He scanned the blinking star chart as the lights flickered on and off, searching for the nearest place he could land that wasn't a Kronock planet. The last thing he wanted was to be floating dead in space. Kronock space.

He swallowed hard and tasted blood, a parting gift from the Kronock fighters, he was sure. He rubbed his chin and shifted in his seat. At least nothing was broken, and he hadn't been shot. He touched his fingertips to the scorched fabric on his shoulder and amended his assessment—not shot badly. He stole a glance at Bridget next to him. She looked to be in one piece, even if her shoulder-length, black hair was disheveled, and there were smudge marks on her face. He noticed a tiny cut on her neck, confirmation the enemy had removed her tracker. Luckily for him, not quickly enough.

Up until that point, he'd been focused on getting his younger brother married and then focused on getting off the

Kronock research facility in one piece. He hadn't spent too much time considering Bridget. She'd been the pretty tribute bride promised to a fellow Drexian warrior, and the woman he'd escorted back to her suite when she'd had one too many cocktails at the tiki bar. She'd also been off-limits for more reason than one.

It was hard to deny she was beautiful, and he recalled reading she'd been a performer on Earth. A dancer. Now that he'd been around her it made sense. Kax had been impressed the female had kept up with him, and thrown a few serious kicks of her own. She was tougher than her willowy body would have led him to believe, although he hadn't been able to miss that she had curves where it counted.

He felt the heat rising in his body, as he thought back to her taking off her dress and exposing her pert, round breasts, the light-brown nipples small and hard. He reminded himself that this female was not for him. Even if her original mate had been killed in battle, she would be matched to a virile Drexian. Not one who was damaged goods, like him. She'd be taken care of back at the station. He swallowed the taste of blood and focused on the readouts.

If he got her back to the station, he thought, his eyes taking in the limited options on the screen. They were far from safe, and he suspected the Kronock would be coming after them very quickly. Something in the face of the alien commander told him this was about more than provoking a battle, and that made his stomach clench.

He and Dorn had arranged a rendezvous point as well as a dedicated and secure communications channel, but it looked like his communication systems were fried, and they would never make it to the rendezvous point at this rate. Dorn wouldn't be able to locate them using Bridget's tracker, either, since that was now gone. Luckily, Kax had sent the station the coordinates of Choor Dar during his approach. At least that was something.

"So what's the verdict?" Bridget asked, her face searching his.

"We aren't going to crash," Kax said. "That's the good news. The bad news is we can't coast forever. Right now, we still have one functioning engine, but once that goes we'll be sleeping ducks."

"Sleeping ducks?" Bridget asked, cocking one eyebrow, the edge of her mouth quirking up.

"Isn't that an Earth expression? Like sleeping ducks?"

Her face broke into a smile. "I think you mean sitting ducks."

"Oh." He returned her smile. "Then we will be sitting ducks."

"That's not good." Bridget's smile faded.

Kax didn't want to tell her they couldn't send out an SOS. Their best bet was to try to evade their enemy and hide out until the Drexians could come for them. Dorn would come as soon as Kax didn't make the rendezvous. Knowing his impatient brother, he might not wait that long. Kax was counting on it.

Engaging the engines at maximum thrust, he set a course for the nearest planets. Maybe they could hide out while he tried to repair the ship, although his mechanic skills were even rustier than his field skills. "If we can make it that far, there's an abandoned mining colony," he said, clearing his throat. "Our intelligence shows the Kronock stripped it bare years ago, but it's the best chance we have."

"I'm just glad to be out of there and away from them." Bridget shivered and rubbed her arms through the environmental suit she still wore, which was now black against the dark copilot chair. "Thanks for coming for me. Alone." Her mouth quirked at the corner. "You're either really brave or really stupid."

Kax noticed her half smile and gave her one of his own. "Or my sister-in-law was very convincing."

"Mandy," Bridget said, letting out a breath. "Are she and Dorn okay? Did those alien creeps hurt anyone when they kidnapped me?"

"Everyone's fine," he said. "There was no attack. Do you remember anything about when you were taken?"

Bridget rubbed her head. "Nothing. A pain in my neck, and then nothing. When I woke up, I was in a cell of some kind on a ship. I could feel we were moving, so I figured it was a small transport ship."

Kax nodded to keep her talking.

"The big alien in the black armor told me they needed my DNA to enhance their biodiversity and make it easier to invade Earth. He also told me he's called Krav."

"Krav," Kax repeated, swinging his head around. "He said that? They're going to invade Earth?"

Bridget bobbed her head up and down. "Yep. Apparently if they add Earth DNA to theirs it will make it easier to assimilate our people. Something like that."

Kax let out a slow breath as he thought. This was worse than he'd expected. Not only were the Kronock more advanced than they'd led everyone to believe, it appeared they had a master plan. A plan that included invading Earth and, if past invasions were any indication, harvesting all natural resources and inhabitants. The knot in Kax's stomach tightened. Not only would this mean the end of Earth, it would mean the end of the Drexians, since the treaty with Earth and the tribute brides were the only way his species had continued to thrive.

"Kax?" Bridget touched his arm. "Did you hear me? Are you okay?"

He jerked back, feeling the warmth from her touch spread through him. "I'm fine. I'm trying to process what you told me. Did he say anything else about the invasion? How or when?"

She returned her hand to the armrest. "No. That was it. I told him I had no intention of giving him my DNA and he jabbed me with another needle and knocked me out." She pulled her arms around herself. "The next time I woke up, I was naked on a hard metal table, with tubes in my arms and feet."

He tried to push aside any thoughts of her naked body, even though he felt his cock twitch. "But when I found you, you were dressed and roaming the halls."

She straightened her shoulders. "I wouldn't say 'roaming the halls.' I was looking for a way out, and I had a weapon. I was also barely clothed. They ruined my dress." Bridget managed a small smile. "Let's just say the Kronock underestimated me."

"I'd say so." Kax remembered the kick to his midsection. "You're a lot tougher than you look."

"You have no idea," Bridget said, her smile slipping. She took a deep breath. "So what's your plan to stop it?"

"To stop what?" Kax asked.

"The invasion, of course. I may never get to return to Earth, but I don't want it taken over by asshole aliens like the Kronock." She slapped her hands on the armrests of her chair. "What's your plan to stop them from destroying my people?"

Kax eyed her. She had spirit, for sure. "My mission is to get you back to the station. Then, I can share what you know with the High Command and determine our next moves."

Bridget frowned. "How long will that take? They could be launching an attack now."

"My first priority is not to get caught by the Kronock. If

they think they need human DNA for their invasion, keeping you from them is crucial."

That seemed to pacify her. She gave a small nod. "I'm all for that. I did not like the way that big alien looked at me."

Kax had seen the way the creature had looked at her, as well. If he didn't think the Kronock were emotionless monsters, he'd have thought it was lust. There was no doubt it was desire, whether the desire went beyond acquiring her DNA, he couldn't be sure. One thing he knew, he had to keep her out of Kronock hands. He felt his own hands curling into fists as he thought about the Kronock touching her. The idea of those cold-blooded, mutated creatures laying a single clawed finger on her made his blood boil. He would never let that happen again, even if it meant dying in the process. Even if it meant he was only saving her to be with another Drexian.

"You wouldn't happen to have anything else I could wear?" Bridget asked after a minute of silence.

He looked over at the black suit. The thin fabric was incredibly strong and designed for resilience, but he doubted it was comfortable without anything on underneath. "There may be something in the wall panel behind you."

Bridget rose and moved a few feet back to open the storage panel of the shuttle. "Wow. There's a little bit of everything in here." She held up a shiny, sealed pouch. "Are these MREs?"

"I do not know 'MREs,' but they are travel rations."

She nodded. "MREs. I dated a Marine once."

Kax knew Marines were a type of Earth warrior, and he felt his stomach twist again. He knew he had no right to feel anything close to jealousy. His mission was to return her so she could be matched with another Drexian. End of story.

She tossed the packet into her seat and pulled out a black, short-sleeved shirt worn under military uniforms. "A T-shirt. Now this is what I'm talking about."

Kax twisted around to see what she called a T-shirt as she unzipped the flight suit and stepped out of it. He meant to turn back around right away but was transfixed by the sight of her naked body—all long, sinewy limbs, with a firm ass and high, rounded breasts. His cock hardened as she pulled the shirt over her head, and he turned back before she caught him gaping at her with raw desire. He forced the feeling down, closing his eyes and fighting for control. *She's not yours. She can never be yours.*

"Much better." Bridget scooped up the rations and flopped back in the chair, her muscular legs bare. Tearing open the packet, she sniffed it before pulling out the slab of Drexian flat-bread and taking a bite. She swallowed and held it out to Kax. "Want some?"

He shook his head, avoiding glancing over at Bridget. Even though the Drexian-sized shirt reached halfway down her thighs, Kax knew she had nothing on underneath it, and he forced himself to focus on the readouts.

"It's not bad." She took another bite, then leaned closer to him. "You sure you don't want to get out of your jumpsuit? I promise I won't peek."

He shook his head without looking at her. The less he looked at her, the better.

CHAPTER NINE

Bridget tried not to be offended when he wouldn't meet her eyes. She'd thought this guy had a sense of humor, but apparently not. "Just a joke," she mumbled, more to herself than anything else.

Kax glanced over at her. "It will be a while until we reach our destination. You should get some rest."

Her first instinct was to protest, but as soon as he mentioned sleep she felt the exhaustion of the day wash over her. She didn't know if it was the dull hum of the ship's engine, or the fact that the adrenaline pumping through her body was wearing off, but she was suddenly bone tired.

She finished off the flatbread, then craned her neck to inspect the small craft. "You hiding a bed in here somewhere?"

"Actually. . ." He stood and flipped a few levers on the wall, and a single bunk flipped down from the middle. "There's one on each side."

She gave an appreciative nod. "Pretty clever. It's like one of those train compartments."

"What is a train?" He returned to his pilot's chair, and

watched as she sat on the bunk and bounced up and down gently a few times.

"Do you not have trains on your home world?" She made the motions with her hands as though she were pushing a toy train. "You know, things that have lots of cars and roll around on metal rails."

"Sounds primitive," he said.

"Well, excuse me. I guess we can't all be technologically advanced super-aliens." She put a hand over her mouth to cover a yawn.

"I never said the Drexians were 'super aliens,' although we are known throughout the galaxy as fierce warriors. We just happen to have more advanced technology than your planet."

"Yeah, these suits that change color are pretty cool." She motioned to his arm.

"Drexians are known for stealth technology in many forms."

She watched him swivel back around to the console. Even though she was sleepy, she didn't want him to stop talking. The sound of his deep voice kept her mind off what had happened over the past day, and prevented her from thinking about what might happen if they got caught. "Tell me about growing up Drexian. What was it like to have Dorn as a brother?"

He let out a snort of laughter and twisted back around. "Infuriating. He was a daredevil, and was always coming up with some plan that got us both in trouble."

Bridget smiled as she lay down on the bunk. "Now that I can believe." She propped herself up by one elbow. "So tell me about your home planet. Is it mostly water, like Earth?"

He shook his head. "We have many high mountains, with cities occupying the valleys. Some rivers and lakes, but no vast oceans. We also have less gravity than you do."

"Really? But it feels the same on the station." She looked him up and down. "Is that why you guys are so much taller and bigger than humans?"

"Maybe. We've adjusted the gravity to suit you, but we are used to much less," he said. "We thought having human females floating around would not be the best idea."

"Oh, I don't know." She winked at Kax. "I can imagine some fun things to do in zero gravity."

His cheeks colored, and he spun back to the console.

She let out a breath. "I'm only kidding around. I promise I'm not trying to hit on you. I know I'm matched up with another Drexian. I'm just a naturally flirty person, that's all. I'm not serious about it. " She flopped down on the bunk. "Plus, I like to see a big tough guy like you get all flustered."

He cleared his throat. "I should focus on getting you back to the Boat safely. We are still several parsecs away from the nearest habitable planet."

"So I know Mandy was a big reason you came to get me, but why you?"

He looked at her over his shoulder. "What do you mean? You wish it had been someone else?"

"No." Bridget rolled over so she was leaning on both elbows. "But I know you're a Drexian big shot, and a rescue mission isn't something a politician on Earth would do. They'd send a soldier."

"I was a soldier," he said. "Before I took my father's seat on the High Command. Every Drexian is trained as a warrior, and my specialty was military intelligence."

Her eyebrows popped up. "You're a spy?"

"*Was* a spy." He paused for a moment, considering. "I suppose I am again, since I gave my seat on the High Command to Dorn and am returning to field work."

"So now Dorn has to stay put and be a big shot, and you get

to fly all over being a hero? I'll bet your brother loved that when you told him."

Kax smiled wryly. "He does not know he will need to sit on the High Command yet. I doubt he will be amused."

"There's an understatement," Bridget mumbled.

"He hates the idea of being away from the battle, but he won't let our family down."

"Drexians are big on honor and family, I take it."

Kax didn't say anything for a while. "Those are probably the most important things to a Drexian. Your honor and your family name. Dorn and I are from House Baraat, which is one of the original ruling families. Only members of the ruling families can sit on the High Command."

"So if you aren't from a good family, you're screwed?" Bridget asked, frowning.

Kax gave her a perplexed look. "Screwed? As in. . .?"

"As in, you can never make it if you aren't born important."

"No," he shook his head, looking down at the console as a light blinked red. "Any warrior can achieve greatness by excelling in battle. We have many commanders and captains who did not come from ruling families. The greatest honor for a Drexian is to be a great warrior, not to sit around a table with a bunch of old men."

Bridget relaxed. "That's good. I wouldn't like to think I was marrying into a society that only rewarded the rich and powerful."

He rotated his chair around. "You did not react like Mandy to the idea of being a tribute bride."

"You mean, I didn't threaten to sue you and pitch a fit?" Bridget smiled thinking of the scene her friend had made when told she was being mated to an alien. "It's not really my style, although I enjoyed watching Mandy tell you guys where you could shove it."

Kax blinked quickly a few times, clearly confused.

"It's an Earth expression," she said, giving a small laugh at his perplexed expression. "It means she wasn't going to go along with it."

"Ah," he said. "No, it took her a while to decide to accept Dorn. What made you decide to agree to the terms even before you saw your intended mate?"

She yawned and lay down on her back, looking up at the shuttle ceiling and not meeting Kax's eyes. It would be easier to be honest if she wasn't looking at him. "I guess I'm not the romantic she is."

"Romantic?"

Bridget stared up at the shiny metal of the ceiling. "She probably assumed she'd be swept off her feet by some sweet, gorgeous guy one day, and fall head over heels in love. I'll bet Mandy has planned her wedding since she was a kid, and imagined walking down the aisle a thousand times. I'm not like that. I never have been. After my family died, I was always too busy surviving to think about things like weddings. There's no place in your life for fate or romance or true love when it doesn't matter in the long run." She steadied her breath. "Love never did me any good, so it isn't something I'm looking for. It honestly doesn't matter to me if I marry a Drexian warrior or a human or no one at all. I decided to marry a Drexian, because being one of your people's tribute brides seems like a better gig than living with the women who rejected their matches. At least this way, I get a lot of cool perks. The only downside is I have to plan a wedding, and the wedding planners you guys have are a little intense."

Bridget paused for air when she was done, afraid to look at Kax's reaction to her confession. She'd never said what she felt out loud, but it felt good to tell someone.

"The Gatazoids are known for being perfectionists," Kax

said. "That's why they are our artisans and chefs and wedding planners. Serge is a Gatazoid, which is why he is, as you say, intense."

Bridget twisted to look at Kax but he was facing forward again. Was that all he was going to say about her spilling her guts?

"I'm sorry you lost your family," he added, his voice soft. "I understand loss, and your life not being what you'd hoped."

Bridget felt tears spring to her eyes and she looked up and rapidly blinked to stem their flow. She never cried anymore. Not even when she'd been cut by the ballet, so what was going on now? She pressed the heels of her hands into her eyes. It must have been the stress of the day catching up with her.

She turned onto her back again, and one tear snaked down the side of her face. "Thanks."

"You should rest," he said. "It could be a while before we land."

Bridget glanced at Kax's broad back one last time, before letting her eyes close. For some reason, she felt safer than she had in years. Even though she was in a damaged shuttle, wearing nothing but an oversized shirt, with terrifying aliens chasing after her, she felt like everything was going to be okay. She smiled as she let the vibration of the ship lull her quickly to sleep.

CHAPTER TEN

Kax breathed in and out slowly, practicing the exercises he'd been taught to keep his heart rate steady in battle. He inhaled the breath into his body, feeling it fill his chest and then he held it for a beat, releasing it out his mouth in a slow stream. He uttered a curse when he felt the bulge still pressing against his leg, held tight by the snug suit. So much for a warrior's self-control, he thought, as he fought to keep from looking at the female asleep behind him.

Bridget had been sleeping for a while, and he'd gotten used to the tiny noises she made in her sleep—breathy sighs and moans. What he hadn't adjusted to was the bit of her high, round ass that was exposed since she'd turned over and tucked her arms under her head, the shirt riding up and revealing all of her legs and the bottom half of her ass cheeks. After he'd first twisted around to check on her and gotten a glimpse, he hadn't looked again, but knowing she lay so close to him and so bare had made concentration impossible.

Get a hold of yourself. She can never be yours.

He thought about what she'd told him. She'd never really belong to anyone. Not her heart, at least. His mind went to the Drexian who had been matched to her and then killed in battle. He wondered who would replace him. There was a waiting list for brides, so no doubt it would be another worthy warrior. He felt a pang for her future mate, both jealousy that it would be another Drexian matched with the beautiful, alluring female, and pity, since, according to Bridget, she would never form an attachment to anyone again.

After seeing how his brother was with his new mate, he couldn't imagine spending a life with a female who didn't feel that level of passion. He and Dorn had both lived with a detached and emotionally distant father, and they hadn't known their mother, who'd died while in childbirth with Dorn. He knew the pain of never feeling loved. He would not wish it on anyone, and he would never want to feel that again.

Kax realized his heart rate had returned to normal and the hard bulge in his pants had relaxed. Just in time. Another glance at the console told him they were approaching the planet with the former mining colony. Kax dropped them down to one-quarter power as the orange orb came into view, reddish cloud cover swirling over its surface.

"Let's see what's left down there," he murmured.

Bridget stirred behind him, no doubt wakened by the shift in the ship's engine, and the slight rattling as they approached the planet. "Where are we?"

"We're at the planet I mentioned," he said, without taking his eyes off their descent. "The one with the abandoned mining colony."

Bridget joined him at the console and strapped herself in, as the shuttle entered the planet's atmosphere, the hull trembling. The air was thick and hazy, and lightning shot through the fog around them. He noticed she was clutching the armrests. "Nice vacation spot."

He knew she was trying to lighten the mood, but he was too busy trying to steady their descent to reply. It felt like they were flying through a storm, but there was no rain. Even though the atmosphere was dense and the air an orange-red, murky soup, he was able to locate the remains of an old village and a cluster of buildings that looked habitable on his sensors. No life forms, but the lightning could be disrupting his readouts.

He flew over a small range of hills, noticing the planet had little to no vegetation. No surprise, considering the air quality. He wondered if it had always been this way. Kax steadied the ship, as he eyed a flat expanse to the south of the buildings and engaged the landing gear.

The vessel touched down with a jolt that made his head slam against the back of his chair. Cutting the engine, he turned to Bridget. "You okay?"

She held out her fist and stuck her thumb up.

He'd take that as a yes. He peered out the front of the ship, squinting to see the buildings through the haze and flashes of lightning. "We can wait out the storm in the ship, or make a run for it."

Bridget followed his line of sight. "What are we hoping is in the buildings?"

"This used to be a mining colony that was part of a galaxy-wide network, so I'm hoping the communications systems are still in place. Not to mention, the chance that there might be something that could help me repair our engine."

"Any chance of a hot shower?" Bridget asked with a grin. "Maybe a bubble bath?"

"Slim," he said.

Her grin widened. "Slim is not none." She stood up. "I'll take it."

"Let's pack the rations," he said, joining her and opening his now-empty pack. He avoided staring at her long legs as she helped him fasten the bunk back into the wall and empty the contents of the storage unit into his pack, which he then swung onto one shoulder.

Bridget picked up the black environmental suit she'd left in a heap on the floor. "I guess I need this again." She sighed and stepped into it, flipping the hood up over her head.

He glanced back at the controls to make sure he'd powered down and locked all the systems, when he saw a flash of movement near the closest building. He blinked hard, but it was gone.

"I must be seeing things," he muttered to himself as he scoured the murky landscape and saw no movement. "This place is deserted."

"I hope you're right."

Her nervous voice made him hesitate. No, he told himself, this was their best option. They needed to get a message to his people, and floating around space in a damaged ship with no light-speed or jump capability made them easy prey. He spun on her. "You stay behind me and follow my orders, okay?"

She bobbed her head up and down, her own expression solemn. "I'll do exactly what you tell me to."

He thought of her following orders having nothing to do with getting to the building, and he jerked his eyes away from her face with a grunt. He flipped his hood up and sealed it, and she did the same.

Opening the shuttle door, Kax stepped out and Bridget followed him. Now that they were outside, he could feel the heat of the air and the force of the wind. He hadn't seen any indications the colony was inhabited, but not being able to see anything or get clear readings made him wary. His senses were on high alert, and he unhooked the blaster from his belt.

After pressing his wrist controller to close the door, Kax began trudging toward the nearest building, keeping Bridget behind him with one arm and holding his blaster out with the other. The roar of the wind made it impossible to hear anything, and the churning air slammed against him from all sides. He focused on staying upright and moving forward. He had to get them inside the building before they were blown away.

He caught a flash of movement out of the corner of his eye, and he fired out of instinct. More laser fire came their way, and he pushed Bridget to the ground, his heart hammering in his chest. So much for the planet being uninhabited and the colony deserted. Clearly, someone was here, and whoever it was wasn't happy to see them.

His body was pressing against hers as he pinned her to the ground, but he couldn't allow himself to think about anything but keeping her safe. Peering through the storm, he saw a blink of red and fired again, seeing something drop. He paused, waiting for more blaster fire to come. Nothing.

He shifted slightly but didn't get up. Kax found it hard to believe there was only one hostile. Where there was one enemy, there were usually many. When another few seconds passed with no weapons fired, he pushed himself off Bridget, pulling her up with him as he stood. Their suits had morphed to match the environment, so she looked like a red-orange outline. Since the wind still screeched around them, he couldn't ask if she was okay, but he met her eyes through the clear masks and gave her the okay hand signal he'd seen humans use. She nodded and gave him the okay signal back.

He realized he was practically standing on top of her, so he stepped back and turned toward the building, pulling her close behind him. Knowing the colony wasn't completely deserted made him even more cautious as he moved forward, his head swiveling from side to side as he tried to catch any more movement. Where were the rest of the inhabitants? There had to be more than one.

As they got closer to the building, he saw the figure he'd shot. His chest constricted. It was Kronock. He edged forward, a feeling of dread overtaking him as he realized that wasn't exactly true. The legs and arms had the familiar scales of his enemy, but the trunk of the creature looked entirely robotic, as did the machinery encasing his head. Instead of the one red eye he'd seen on the Kronock fighters, this version of his enemy had two mechanical eyes and held only a scant trace of the organic being. The circuitry on the alien's chest looked charred—no doubt from his blaster fire—and the flashing red eyes he'd seen through the swirling haze were no longer illuminated.

Kax felt Bridget clasp his arm as she stared down at the dead creature. He put a hand on hers to reassure her, even though he felt a growing panic. He didn't have time to think about what these half machine Kronock meant, or how many they'd built. One fact filled his head—the Kronock would not have left just one soldier behind. There were more, even if he couldn't see them yet.

He turned to signal Bridget they should go back to the ship when he felt an impact to his chest followed by a burning sensation. Out of instinct, he twisted and fired at the flash, seeing the red lights drop through the fiery haze before the roar of the wind became a roar inside his head, and he fell to his knees.

CHAPTER
ELEVEN

Bridget screamed as she saw Kax fire his weapon and then collapse, but the storm swallowed her sound. The figure that'd shot him lay unmoving on the ground, but Bridget kept it in her sights as she knelt beside Kax.

She couldn't tell if he was breathing through his face mask, so she pressed her fingers against the side of his neck and felt grateful the suit's fabric was thin. There was a faint pulse, although it seemed erratic.

Looking around, she saw nothing but red haze. If there were any other enemies with blasters, she couldn't see them, although an army could be approaching and she wouldn't be able to hear it over the wailing wind. The only sound as loud as the wind was the sound of her own heartbeat pounding in her ears. It wasn't so much fear for herself that had her heart racing as fear for Kax. He'd taken blaster fire fully on the chest, and she didn't know if it was like being shot with a gun or like being shot with a Taser. Either way, he wasn't moving and she needed to get him inside.

"Let's go," she muttered as she tucked his blaster under her arm, hooked her elbows under the Drexian's armpits, and began dragging him, stopping once to readjust her grip.

When she reached the side of the nearest building, she propped him against her legs as she tried to open the door. Luckily, it had a handle. Unfortunately, the handle was locked and no amount of jiggling would budge it.

She slammed the palm of her hand against the metal door as it held firm. "Son of a . . ."

Bridget considered going back to the ship, but she knew they needed to get a signal out to the Drexians, and now she needed to treat Kax's wound. Plus, she didn't know if she could drag Kax all the way back to the ship without them being shot at again.

Crouching low, she hurried the few feet to the alien they'd left lying face up on the ground. Her stomach clenched at the sight of the metal grafted to gray scales, and she tried not to think how the Kronock had turned their own people into robots.

Bridget averted her gaze from his mechanical face as she patted him down. He must have keys or a remote control, or anything that might get her inside. Nothing. She felt like kicking him as she stood up again. If he was outside, he had to have a way to get back in. He was near the door when he'd shot at them.

She bent down again and rolled him slightly in case he was lying on top of something. His arm flopped down with the palm facing up, and Bridget saw a circle of blue light blinking in the center of his mechanical, clawed hand.

"This had better work," she said, as she tugged him by the arm to the door, lifted his blinking hand to the round panel beside it, and pressed it as hard as she could.

The panel glowed blue, the latch snapped open, and the handle snapped down automatically. "Bingo."

Bridget rolled the Kronock out of the way and pulled Kax inside the building, pressing the door shut behind them. The sound of the wind died out and she unzipped her hood, taking a tentative breath and finding the air in the dark hallway to be clean if a little stale. She knew Kax had said the colony had been abandoned and scans showed no life forms, but the presence of the Kronock made her nervous. Since the creatures outside were more robot than living being, would they have registered on a sensor? And if not, did that mean there could be more?

Hearing nothing, she dragged Kax down the narrow passageway until she found a room that held a set of bunk beds. Very long, skinny bunk beds, which made her wonder what kind of creatures had lived there. She lifted him one end at a time onto the lowest bed and a puff of dust rose from the thin mattress. Maybe the colony truly was uninhabited, and the Kronock had left some security guards, of sorts. Since they weren't living, breathing creatures, maybe they could be left alone for years.

She unzipped Kax's hood and began to tug his suit off to get a better look at his injury. She was reassured by the rise and fall of his chest, although her breath caught when she pulled off his shirt and got a glimpse of his hard muscles. For a guy who served on the High Command, he was ripped. She couldn't resist running her fingers down the swell of his chest and the rippled surface of his stomach. She knew he'd recoil from her touch if he was conscious, but she couldn't resist touching him, even though she felt guilty as she did it.

It was obvious he didn't really like her. He avoided looking at her, he flinched at her touch, and he didn't seem to be affected by her flirting. Even when they'd been the maid of honor and best man in Mandy and Dorn's wedding, he'd been cordial but not overly friendly. Too bad for him, she thought, because he was exactly her type.

Her hands lingered on the scorch mark high on his chest near his shoulder. The skin wasn't broken, but it looked burned and felt hot. He moaned as she touched it, and she snatched her fingers away as if she'd been burned.

At least he was alive, she thought, glad he hadn't caught her feeling him up. That would be a tough one to explain, since she was technically promised to another Drexian. Not that she'd met the warrior she'd been matched with, she reasoned. Was it possible to cheat on someone you'd never met? If you'd asked the guy who was supposed to be on his way to marry her, the answer would probably be yes. Anyway, she wasn't a cheater. Never had been. She'd been cheated on, though, which was part of the reason she despised the idea. Even if she didn't believe in love, she did believe in honesty.

She stepped back from Kax as he lay on the bed, his chest bare and his suit pulled down to his hips. "I'm going to go look for... something that might help."

She knew he couldn't hear her, but she had to break the ominous silence of the room that had been untouched for years. She pulled off her own suit and crept down the hallway in the oversized black T-shirt, noticing more rooms with elongated bunk beds to her right and left. The building must have been a barracks of some sort back when the mining colony had been operational. She peered into a larger room with a pair of armless, beige couches and tall, straight-backed chairs hunched around square tables. Something that looked like game pieces with unusual markings on them lay scattered across one table, as if the game had been interrupted.

Farther down the hall, Bridget found a galley kitchen. After opening the high cabinets, she determined whatever food had once been there was now gone. Only a few dusty and empty boxes remained on the shelves. She pushed a button next to the faucet, and after a moment's hesitation, water shot out—first brown, and then clear. She grabbed a cloth from a peg and soaked it with cold water, enjoying the feeling as the liquid spilled over her hands.

She ran back down the hall with the dripping towel and pressed it to Kax's burned chest. He inhaled sharply, his brows furrowing, and let out a long breath. Bridget felt the cool cloth absorbing the heat of his wound. When the fabric was warm, she hurried back down the hall and soaked it again, returning to press it on the blast mark and absorb the heat, then doing this several more times until Kax's skin no longer burned.

He made soft noises, his eyelids fluttering, and Bridget took this as a good sign. "Thank you for not leaving me here alone," she whispered, as she removed the cloth from his chest and noticed the scorch mark was lighter. "I'm used to being alone in the world. Doesn't mean I like it."

He moved one hand so it rested on her bare leg as she sat next to him. His voice was faint and husky. "I would never leave."

Bridget froze, the wet cloth in one hand dripping water on his chest as he slid his hand farther up her bare leg. She was suddenly very aware she had nothing on underneath the big T-shirt. As far as she could tell, he was still out of it. His eyes were closed, and his breath was slow and steady.

He murmured something unintelligible and moved his hand up. Any farther and he would be able to feel how wet she was. Bridget stood quickly and let his hand drop, backing out of the room and rushing down the hall. She returned to the galley kitchen, dropping the damp cloth in the sink and leaning against it with both hands.

What was that? Kax must have been dreaming and

thought she was somebody else. She knew he wouldn't hit on her if he was conscious. She was promised to another Drexian, and Kax was all about honor. Plus, he wasn't into her. Aside from the little he'd told her in the shuttle, she didn't know much about Dorn's brother. As far as she knew he wasn't married, and didn't have a tribute bride waiting for him. She snorted. If he wasn't into humans, maybe he was dreaming about a sexy alien with three breasts, or something.

She'd heard whispers on the Boat that Drexian females looked different than humans—taller, more muscular, more breasts. Of course, that had been back when there were available Drexian females. None had been born in a generation, which was why the tribute bride program had been created in the first place. Not that every Drexian wanted a human mate. She knew some opted to remain single. She wondered if Kax was one of those who didn't find humans attractive. It would explain why he flinched at her touch. Too bad for her because he was hot as hell, and she hadn't been with a man in so long she was afraid she'd forgotten how.

"Get it together, Bridget," she whispered, pressing the button for the water and letting it run. It had clearly been a long time, considering how fast she revved up when he touched her. Even thinking about the feel of his hand on her leg made her body warm with desire. She hung over the sink, her head near the rushing water—the sound calming her.

She pressed the button again to stop the water, picked up the towel, and turned to the door, screaming when she saw the hulking Kronock standing in the hall. She let the towel fall to the floor with a wet splat.

So much for there being only the outside sentries. She backed up as it took a step toward her, the clawed feet echoing off the tile.

"You are unauthorized," it said in a halting, mechanical voice. "This colony is off limits. You are unauthorized."

"Okay," she said. "I get it. I'm not authorized." Her back touched the wall, and she wished she hadn't left Kax's blaster back in the room.

CHAPTER TWELVE

Kax's head swam as he forced his eyes to open. He blinked a few times, his blurred vision coming into focus. Instead of peering through the fiery-red storm, he seemed to be in a dimly lit room, looking up at the underside of a bed. He rolled onto his side and felt a hard mattress beneath him. He breathed in and smelled dust, coughing as his movement sent up a cloud from the bed. He wasn't on the shuttle and he wasn't back at the Drexian space station. Where was he?

The last thing he remembered was coming out of the ship and heading toward one of the buildings then seeing something move in the distance. He raised a hand to his bare chest, remembering firing and then being fired on. He felt the tender skin where he'd been hit, but it was also strangely wet and cool to the touch. Looking down at his naked chest, he vaguely recalled a female's voice as she pressed something cold to his wound. She'd been talking to him. What had she said?

His head throbbed as he sat up. Bridget. The tribute bride he'd rescued from the Kronock. The beautiful, dark-haired girl with the warm, brown eyes. That must have been the voice he'd heard, but where was she?

He picked up his blaster from the floor and stood, taking a breath to steady himself. His head swam, and he clutched the bed railing for balance. It looked like he was in a barracks. It reminded him of the Drexian military academy—spartan and spare, although all the furniture looked stretched out. Unless that detail was just his vision playing tricks on him. Nothing like the modern Kronock outpost where he'd located Bridget.

He found that reassuring. Even though he remembered the creature he'd fired on had been Kronock, and a Kronock who was more machine than animal, he didn't see evidence of his enemy inhabiting the building. He knew it couldn't be safe if they'd been shot at, but it was also obvious no one was living there. At least, no one who liked to clean.

He stepped into the hallway—high ceilings, bare walls, and no natural light. Overhead lights flickered, giving the hallway an ominous feel, and the tile beneath his feet was dingy. From the thin coating of dirt on the floor, he could see small footprints leading away from the door and down the hall. Before he could call out for Bridget, a metallic clicking made him whip his head around.

A Kronock—with mechanical, red eyes and metal circuitry all over his body—haltingly raised an arm as Kax fired on him. One metallic hand flew off and then he jerked back as Kax shot into his chest. The creature collapsed, his circuitry spluttering.

Another one appeared behind the pile of broken machinery, and Kax blew its head off before it could advance on him. He paused to regroup and looked at the broken Kronock. These were unlike the fighters they'd encountered during the incursion, and he wondered if they were an early model, or a special sentry variation designed to guard and not necessarily battle.

These had been much easier to defeat, for which he was grateful.

Seeing them lying in a heap of metal and scales made his mind race. He wondered how many of these were spread throughout the galaxy. Were they a beta version of the only slightly augmented fighters he'd battled during the invasion, or had they created many different models? He cringed at the thought of these creatures being assembled in mass numbers—organic parts fused with mechanical ones.

Kax's heart pounded as he prodded at the broken fighters with one foot, and a jolt of pain shot through his chest, reminding him of his wound. He'd been lucky these were slow-moving fighters, since his own movements felt sluggish. Kax knew he had to find Bridget before more Kronock—faster Kronock—found them first. He hoped these were guards left behind and weren't part of a larger fighting force, but he couldn't be sure.

He heard a scream, and spun to see one of the hulking robot creatures at the far end of the hall. It disappeared through a doorway, and Kax ran as quickly as he could, his gait jerky and his breathing labored. A twinge in his chest made him stagger against the wall, catching himself with one arm and pushing himself to keep going.

He saw little but the back of the massive metal creature when he reached the doorway, but he saw a flash of bare leg through the Kronock's own thick, scaly ones. Bridget.

Grek. He felt a surge of anger as the Kronock raised an arm, and Kax fired into its back until it dropped. He leaned one hand against the doorframe as his rush of anger subsided and the pain in his chest and head returned. Bridget stared at him, her eyes wide and her mouth open. He tried to smile at her.

She rushed forward and slipped her arm around him,

taking his blaster before he dropped it. “I didn’t know you were awake.”

He looked down at her. “I heard you scream. I heard. . .” His brows pressed together as he studied her face. “Never mind. I must have been dreaming.”

She cleared her throat and looked down. “You were pretty out of it. Why don’t we go back to bed? I mean, get you back to bed?”

He tried to pull away, but his head swam and he sagged against her.

“I won’t bite you,” she said, “but if you don’t let me help you, you’re going to end up on the floor.”

He nodded with a grimace. “I don’t suppose this place has any medical supplies?”

“Not that I’ve found,” she said, her eyebrows popping up when she saw the pile of Kronock at the end of the hall. “I haven’t searched the whole place though. I stopped when I found the kitchen and water for cold compresses.”

Kax touched a finger to his blaster burn. “I remember. . .” But what did he remember? Something about not leaving her and then the feel of her skin. Had he been touching her? He felt his face flush. He hoped he hadn’t done anything he needed to apologize for. He was here to rescue her, nothing more, he told himself.

“Are you in pain?” she asked.

He pressed his lips together. “I wouldn’t say no to some Pirrin.” When he noticed her confused expression, he added, “It’s a Drexian pain medication. Very effective.”

“I’ll have a look around.”

“Let’s look together,” he said. “I don’t like the idea of you wandering around this place by yourself. Who knows how many Kronock there are?”

“I’m pretty sure the Kronock we’ve seen are just security

guards left behind. They aren't as tricked out as the fighters we encountered during the battle."

He was impressed she'd made a similar assessment to his own. That didn't mean he was letting her out of his sight again. "I'm coming with you."

She shrugged. "Suit yourself, tough guy."

He grunted, not feeling very tough at all as she helped him shuffle forward.

They passed more sleeping quarters before reaching a room at the very end of the hall with clear paned double doors that swung open. Unlike the rest of the rooms, this one was well lit with a counter running the perimeter of the room and a single metal bed—long and narrow—in the center. Metal arms extended from the ceiling.

"This must be the medical bay," he said, walking inside and leaning against the counter. He noticed Bridget glance up at the metal arms protruding from the ceiling and shudder. "Are you okay? You're sure you weren't hurt?"

She gave a quick shake of her head. "I'm fine. You're the one who's hurt." She guided him to the bed and helped him hop up, her hands lingering on his bare arms for a moment. "I'm tougher than I look, remember?"

He did remember. He tried to focus on her face, but a wave of pain overtook him, and his vision blurred. He felt her touch on his face, even as his world went dark.

CHAPTER THIRTEEN

Bridget watched for a few moments as his eyes drooped and finally closed. Once she was sure he was out, she stroked a hand down the side of his face. He really was handsome, with a square jaw and very kissable lips. She even liked the scruff he'd let grow. Kax had a more buttoned-up appearance than the wild-haired, warrior look of his brother, but she'd always liked short hair. Too bad he looked at her like she had tentacles growing out of her head. She shrugged to herself. Who knew? Maybe tentacles turned him on.

"Now, if only this place came equipped with a doctor." She started to open drawers in a search for Pirrin, coughing when particles of dust danced in the air.

"I am a doctor."

The voice made her spin around with her finger on the trigger of the blaster, even though it hadn't sounded at all like a Kronock. She didn't see anyone in the room or outside in the hall. Please don't let me be hallucinating, she thought.

"State your medical need."

She wasn't imagining things. The voice was real, and as far as she could tell, it came from overhead. "Who are you?" She spun around as she looked up. "Where are you?"

"I'm the imbedded auditory medical program. I'm designed to operate when there is no medical officer available." The voice paused. "Is that the case?"

"You could say that," Bridget muttered, lowering the blaster. "So you're a computer program?"

"I am artificial intelligence." The voice almost sounded offended. "I am much more sophisticated than a simple program."

"Sorry," Bridget said. "Can you fix Drexians?"

"I contain the medical knowledge for over three hundred species, including Drexians."

"Impressive. Who designed you?"

"I am a creation of Validians. This is their mining colony." A pause. "You are not Validian?"

"Nope. I'm human from planet Earth, and I'm here with a Drexian. He's the one who needs help. He was shot in the chest with a blaster."

"I understand. Is the Drexian lying on the table?" The lights above Kax shone brighter.

Bridget looked at the big alien with his eyes closed and felt her throat constrict. Lying on the metal table, with the scorched blast mark on his chest, he looked almost fragile. She tried to respond, but only a squeak came out.

"I will take that as an affirmative."

A half-moon-shaped bar lowered from above and a beam of blue light began scanning Kax's body, stopping when it reached his waist and the bunched up environmental suit.

"Please remove the extraneous fabric."

"What?" Bridget glanced at the suit that had changed color

again to match the silver of the examination table. "Take it off all the way?"

"If you wish the examination to be most effective." If a machine voice could sound exasperated, this one did.

Bridget hesitated. "For a chest wound?"

"Blaster fire can cause damage through the body. Organic systems are all connected." A pause. "Unless you wish me to cease the examination."

"No, I'll take it off." Bridget felt her heartbeat quicken as she tugged at the bottom half of the suit, pulling it off Kax and revealing a snug pair of black cargo pants underneath. "This too?"

"Affirmative."

Bridget blew out a breath. This was going to take some explaining once he was awake. She fumbled with the buttons of his pants and managed to wiggle them down, trying to ignore the massive bulge beneath a pair of black, second-skin boxer-briefs. Her fingers hummed with energy as they skimmed his skin, and by the time she'd pulled the pants off, she was breathing heavily, and not from the exertion.

"Your heart rate is elevated and your skin is discolored," the AI said. "After I examine the Drexian, I should examine you."

"I'm fine." She fanned herself with one hand and looked away from Kax. "Or I will be in a minute."

Staring at his broad shoulders, corded stomach, and muscular thighs was not helping her restraint. Or helping her remember she was engaged. She repeated the word several times in her head. "He doesn't even like you," she muttered to herself, once her fingers had stopped tingling.

"I do not like you or dislike you," the voice informed her. "I am an artificial intelligence, and incapable of those emotions."

She rolled her eyes and was glad the AI couldn't read facial cues. "I'm not talking about you."

"Very well. Unless you have further *relevant* comments, I will resume the examination."

She ignored his pointed comment. How had she managed to get stuck with a smart-ass, virtual doctor?

The scan resumed, followed by a series of beeps and hums from the machine. The bar dropped lower and a thin arm swung down, administering a shot into Kax's neck and spraying something on his chest. He twitched and then his head lolled to the side.

"What are you doing?" Bridget asked. It suddenly occurred to her the Kronock might have reprogrammed the AI when they invaded the colony.

"Administering both pain medication and antibodies to prevent infection, along with a topical solution to speed skin rejuvenation."

"Oh." Bridget watched as Kax's chest wound faded before her eyes. She stepped closer as the bar lifted back up into the ceiling, and she touched a hand to his smooth chest as the redness vanished.

"Your heart rate is rising again. Are you sure you do not need some medication to cure your erratic cardiac condition?"

She jumped back and shook her head. "No. I promise I don't have cardiac issues."

"As you wish." The overhead light dimmed. "The Drexian will heal. His anatomy is simpler than Validian. He is also shorter and wider."

Short and wide were not two words she'd use to describe any Drexian, much less Kax. The Validians must have been emaciated giants.

"I got that from all the really long beds and high ceilings,"

Bridget said. "You do know the Validians aren't here anymore, right?"

"I am an imbedded auditory medical program." A pause. "Nobody tells me anything."

Bridget almost laughed. "Whoever programmed you gave you some personality."

"Doctor Harimti Vlax. A noted Validian inventor and an acknowledged wit."

"I'll bet," Bridget said under her breath. "Did he give you a name?"

"Why would I need a name?"

"No reason," she said. "I'm Bridget."

"Brid-get," he repeated, stopping between the syllables. "What happened to the Validians?"

"I was hoping you could tell me. We came here trying to escape the Kronock and found they'd destroyed the colony and left behind some robot guards. How long has it been since you were activated?"

"Eleven years and thirteen days, when I was last activated to tend to the wounded after an attack."

Bridget tried not to sound as shocked as she was. "So no living creature has been at this colony for over a decade? That explains the dust."

"Do you have any information about the Validians?" the AI asked.

"Sorry," Bridget said. "I only found out there were alien species about a week ago. I'd never heard of the Drexians or the Kronock, and this is the first I'm hearing about the Validians."

"You did not know there were other forms of life beyond your own?" The computer sounded surprised, and a bit disdainful.

"On my planet, if you believe in aliens, you're the one who's considered crazy."

"Interesting. Will you be considered crazy when you return?"

"I doubt I'll ever go back." Bridget sighed. "But, I probably would."

"I do not have any cures for mental illness, Brid-get. I am sorry."

"Don't sweat it, Al."

"Al?"

"If you're going to call me by my name, I should call you by one, and Doc seems pretty impersonal. I figure you're an AI, so I'll call you Al."

"Are all humans crazy like you, Brid-get?"

"Only the fun ones, Al."

"Is this Drexian one of the fun ones?"

Bridget watched Kax sleeping for a moment. "I don't know. I thought he was an administrator type when I first met him, but he volunteered to come rescue me on his own so I'm not sure what to think." She laid a hand on his shoulder and stared down at the light brown lashes resting against his cheek.

"I'm picking up an elevated heart rate again. Is he the cause of your cardiac issues?"

She pulled her hand back and glared up at the ceiling, wishing there was an actual body she could address instead of a voice. "Even if he was, it wouldn't matter. I'm promised to another Drexian."

"I do not understand 'promised.'"

She ran her fingers through her hair. "I'm what his people call a tribute bride. I'm supposed to marry one of their warriors since they don't have females any more. It was a weird deal Earth made in order to be protected from the Kronock."

"Where is this warrior you are supposed to marry? Why did he not rescue you?"

Bridget folded her arms over her chest. "You ask a lot of questions, Al."

"Dead," Kax murmured from the medical bed. "He's dead."

Her head snapped around and she stared at him. She leaned over his chest. "What did you say?"

His eyes were still closed, but moved rapidly beneath his lids as he muttered. "Dead. Killed in the battle." He dropped his voice as if whispering to someone. "Don't tell Bridget."

She'd never met the Drexian she was supposed to be mated to, but the news still hit her like a punch to the gut. Kax knew he was dead this entire time, and hadn't told her?

"Your shallow breathing indicates possible hyperventilation, Brid-get," the AI said. "I suggest putting your head between your knees."

She decided to take Al's advice, dangling her arms on the floor as she swung over at the waist. So it wasn't his respect for her intended that made Kax avoid touching her, after all. All those times she flirted with him and he'd pulled away or averted his eyes wasn't because he was an honorable guy. He really wasn't attracted to her. She focused on breathing in and out as her cheeks burned with humiliation.

CHAPTER FOURTEEN

Kax turned over and felt the cool sheets shift under his stomach. He must be back on the space station and in his suite. The members of the Drexian High Command had suites for their use when they convened at the station, and although they weren't as luxurious as the fantasy suites designed for the tribute brides, they were still comfortable and spacious. He stretched out his legs and felt them brush against the fabric and then his foot touched another leg, this one soft and smooth.

Or maybe he was on one of the pleasure planets. It had been a while, but he welcomed the feel of the female next to him. His cock swelled, another reminder of how long it had been since he'd had any release.

He rolled over and ran a hand up her leg, feeling the soft swell of her ass as he pushed her garment up. She moaned and he hooked his hand around her waist, pulling her to him until her body was flush against his, his hard cock pressing her bare skin through the thin fabric of his underwear. He lowered his head to her neck and inhaled the light, floral scent. He knew the scent, but from where? His thoughts were still hazy. Somewhere in the recesses of his mind, he wondered where his pants had gone, but the thought drifted away as she made soft noises in response to him.

Kax ran a hand up her flat stomach and cupped one of her breasts, making her rock back into him. He heard his own low growl, then felt her jerk and stiffen. He blinked a few times, moving from his dream to consciousness, and becoming aware he wasn't in his bed on the space station. Or on a pleasure planet. He was, however, holding Bridget in his arms, and his rigid cock was pressing against her.

He rolled away and leapt off the bed, pulling the sheet with him when he saw his erection and dropping it when he saw Bridget lying in bed. Her eyes were wide, and she tugged her shirt down to cover herself.

"What are you. . . ?" he began, then stopped when he heard his accusatory tone. "What am I. . .?" His eyes flew around the spacious room with its dusty, oversized, brown furniture. "Where are we?"

Bridget rubbed her eyes as she sat up. "I managed to locate the manager's quarters. I thought this would be more comfortable than the bunk beds. . . and safer."

"I'm sorry." He crossed his arms over his crotch, pressing down on his erection in hopes it wouldn't be as noticeable. "I didn't mean to. . . I didn't know. . ."

Mottled, red patches appeared on her cheeks. "I know you didn't know it was me. If you had, you never would have touched me, right?" Her eyes narrowed at him. "I'm not your type, or you don't like human women, or maybe you just don't like me?"

She didn't seem angry he'd groped her, but she was definitely angry with him over something. He tried to recall the last thing that had happened between them. Had they argued?

Had he insulted her, or told her he didn't like her? He didn't think so, but why did she look like she wanted to rip his head off?

He looked at the floor; not wanting his face to reveal it had been her he'd been thinking about. "I'm here to rescue you. That's it. You're promised to another."

"Yeah, I got that." She let out a huff of breath. "Only the Drexian I was promised to is dead, isn't he?"

Kax's jaw dropped. How did she know? He put a hand to his head. He must have said something when he'd been out of it. He'd always talked in his sleep, and especially when he was on pain meds. Great. Just great. He met her blazing eyes. "That doesn't change my mission. I still have to get you back to the station so you can be matched up with another warrior."

"But not you." It was a statement, not a question, and he noticed her voice had dropped an octave.

"But not me." The words felt like they'd been ripped out of him, and he couldn't look at her when he said them.

"I don't suppose I have any say in this, do I?"

His mouth felt dry and his heart hammered in his chest. He couldn't tell her what had happened to him and why he could never be with her. He knew how she'd look at him if she knew, and he'd rather die than have her pity him. He picked up the sheet from the floor. "Drexian warriors pick their mates."

"Got it." She spat out the words and got off the bed on the other side. For some reason she sounded more upset now than she had before he'd apologized.

Kax did not understand human females, but he knew he didn't have time to decipher her now. He glanced at the closed door. "One of the last things I remember was fighting a bunch of Kronock. Are there any more?"

"If there are, I haven't seen them, but we're on the top floor so we can see anything coming for us." She crossed to the window stretching across one side of the room, her arms pulled tight across her chest. "That is, if the storm ever stops."

Kax saw nothing but orange whirling fog outside. "How long have I been out?"

"Hours," Bridget said, reaching into one of the backpacks on the floor and tossing him a sealed ration pack. "I've eaten a few of these, but you're probably starving. After Al fixed you up, he told me which room was the largest and pointed me in the direction of a gurney."

Kax nodded. He was hungry. He ripped open the foil pouch and bit off a chunk of padwump jerky, then looked down at the unblemished skin on his chest. There was no remnant of the scorch mark indicating he'd been hit with blaster fire, and the searing pain was gone. "Thank you."

She shrugged without looking around at him. "You would have done the same for me."

He flinched at her cool tone of voice then cocked his head to the side. "Wait. Who's Al?"

"The AI medical program that healed you. Once you get past the fact that he has zero bedside manner, he's not bad company."

Kax had a lot of questions and the list was getting longer by the minute. He took another bite of the salty dried meat and swallowed. "So you got me up here on a gurney?"

Bridget turned to look at him and her voice softened. "It took me a while, but luckily this place has elevators. They aren't fast, and I was terrified the cable would snap because they haven't been used in so long, but it held. Anyway, those bunk bed mattresses suck. Plus, this door has a lock on it for an extra layer of protection from those automatons. I haven't seen any on the upper floors, and don't know how good they are at turning handles."

Kax looked at the door, noting that although it had a lock,

the door itself was only made of wood—something a Kronock could blast through in a few seconds. Still, he had to agree the bed was more comfortable. He thought back to being in bed next to her and then became aware he was virtually naked.

"Since I'm healed, I should find the colony's communications hub." He took the final bite of jerky, as he scanned the floor. "And my clothes."

Bridget pointed to the tall wooden cabinet across from the bed. "I hung them in there. It took so long to get you out of them, I couldn't handle trying to jam you back in."

The idea of Bridget undressing him made his cock twitch, and he spun quickly. He cleared his throat as he opened the cabinet doors and saw his pants and shirt hanging on a pair of pegs. He dressed quickly, keeping his back to her, and hoping she hadn't noticed the effect she had on him.

He regretted the death of the Drexian warrior who'd been matched with Bridget, but felt grateful there wasn't anyone he'd need to apologize to once they got back to the station. Feeling up someone else's tribute bride was grounds for a serious ass kicking. If she was his mate, he would tear any man limb from limb if they laid a hand on her. He felt his anger flare as he thought of anyone touching her. Get used to it, he reminded himself. *She's not yours.*

He glanced over his shoulder at the woman standing at the window with her back to him. Maybe it was for the best since at this point, she didn't even seem to like him.

CHAPTER
FIFTEEN

So that was that, Bridget thought. Drexian warriors picked their mates and he clearly didn't choose her.

She guessed she should be grateful he was honest with her. Other men might have taken advantage of the situation, but he'd made it abundantly clear he had no interest in her. She gave a small shake of her head. It didn't matter. She'd dealt with rejection before. Being a professional dancer meant constant rejection—being passed over as the lead dancer again and again, auditioning for roles that went to other people, and finally being cut from the ballet when they decided she was too old. She was not used to being rejected by men though. Men she'd always been able to charm and seduce.

She snuck a glance at Kax as he pulled on his clothes and then his environmental suit, admiring his firm backside and his broad shoulders. Somehow she couldn't work her magic on this one. At least, not when he was conscious.

Fine, she told herself. *He doesn't want me? Two can play at that game.*

If there was one thing she knew, it was focus. She would

focus on nothing but getting them back to the space station. She looked down at the short bureau underneath the window, running a finger through the layer of dust on top. She began pulling open the drawers, sending the dust spiraling up and making her cough. Just as she'd suspected. The director of the colony had left in a hurry and abandoned drawers full of clothes. She pawed through them until she found dark, draw-string pants.

She pulled them on, tying them as tight as she could and rolling up the extra fabric at her ankles. Baggy, but wearable. She pulled her environmental suit on over the pants, leaving the hood down, and tugged on her boots. She straightened up and saw Kax watching her. "You ready to see the comms station?"

"You know where it is?"

She walked past him, picking up the blaster she'd left on the nightstand and tossing it to him. "I told you Al was helpful. He accessed the colony's computers and showed me the schematics. It's in the next building. The one before you reach the warehouses where most of the sentries are stationed."

"How do you know that?"

Bridget sighed. "Al is part of the colony's computer system, so he can tap into the old security feed. He can also access the sensors that were used to determine levels of metal toxicity in the warehouses."

Kax blinked at her a few times. "Which means...?"

"The Kronock aren't storing metal ore in there anymore. All that's gone. But they are storing some sort of radioactive material."

Kax flinched. "That explains the guards, and why there are no living creatures here."

"Exactly," Bridget said. "So, I say we send out that signal and get off this planet before we start glowing."

She flipped the lock on the door and opened it slowly, peering into the hallway before stepping out. After encountering the Kronock fighters downstairs, she hadn't seen any more, but that didn't mean the ones guarding the warehouses couldn't show up.

Kax pulled her back. "Let me go first."

She put both palms up. "Be my guest, tough guy."

He raised one eyebrow but didn't reply as he proceeded down the corridor with his finger on the trigger of the blaster. They reached the stairs and descended—their footfall echoing in the quiet of the stairwell—until they reached the ground floor. The broken bodies of the Kronock fighters lay scattered in the hall. Even though there was no blood and only the smell of burned wiring, Bridget looked away. She didn't like thinking back to how close she'd come to being shot by one of them.

"Hey," she said, when Kax paused at the door between the buildings. "I never did thank you for shooting that robot before it blew me away."

He gave a small nod. "It wouldn't be much of a rescue if I let you get killed."

"Right. Well, thanks anyway."

He turned and had to look down at her since she was following so close to him. "And thank you for saving me."

She could feel the heat radiating off him and fought the urge put a hand on his arm. "I can't exactly get off this planet without a pilot."

His mouth quirked at the corner. "I guess not."

When he didn't turn back around, she cleared her throat. "There's a covered walkway between the buildings, and the other building is only a few feet away."

He glanced down at their feet and tilted his head. "Feet?"

"Meters, klicks, whatever measurements you use." She waved a hand at the door. "It's really close."

He nodded, flipping up the hood of his suit so it covered his face. "Ready?"

"Ready." She did the same with her environmental suit and waited to breathe in the oxygen flow. She jerked when he took her hand, but he held on as he pushed the door open and rushed outside, pulling her behind him.

The wind howled as it spun around them, but Kax powered across to the other door, tugging it open and pushing her inside ahead of him. The door slammed shut, and the sound of the wind became faint.

Bridget felt a flutter of panic as they stood in the dark, and she groped along the wall for a switch. Nothing. She hated the dark and not knowing what might be waiting for them.

Kax tightened his grip on her hand, rubbing the back of it slowly with his thumb. The pressure calmed her, and she stepped closer to him, liking the feel of his bulk next to her. She also liked that he couldn't see her face in the dark, couldn't see how scared she was. Now that they were inside, she removed her hood, and heard him do the same.

He pulled her into him so her own arm was behind her back and her body was pressed flush against his. He dropped his head, putting his lips right beside her ear. "Shhhhh," he whispered so softly she barely heard him but could feel the vibration against her earlobe. It sent shivers down her spine, and she felt her nipples harden. She managed to nod but didn't reply.

Bridget heard nothing but the sound of her own shallow breathing and Kax's slow steady breaths as they stood in the pitch-black darkness. After a moment, she heard the clang of metal and saw glowing red pinpoints in the distance. Kax tensed and fired. There was a crash, and then more glowing, red lights.

Kax pulled her down with him as he continued to shoot

into the dark, shielding her body with his. She was so close to him, she felt his racing heartbeat as if it were her own. Blaster fire pierced the air above them, illuminating his fierce face for a moment before returning them to darkness. He rolled her so she was laying flat on her back with his body covering hers as he continued to shoot, and Kronock continued to drop. When the firing stopped, there was nothing but the sound of their breathing and the hissing of broken machines.

He'd propped himself on one elbow so he wouldn't crush her, and after a moment he lowered his head to hers. "Are you okay?"

She was shaking, but she wasn't sure if it was just the shock of the battle, or the fact that he lay on top of her and she could feel every rock-hard inch of him. She couldn't see him, but could feel Kax quivering. "Are you?"

He buried his head in her neck and breathed deeply, nodding but not speaking. Bridget raised a hand hesitantly and touched the side of his face. This seemed to snap him into action. He pushed himself up and pulled her with him, jerking them both to standing.

"Each building must have its own group of guards." He kept his voice low. "I don't think they're connected or communicate, otherwise they would have all come looking for us when we were in the other building."

"Did you get all the ones in here?"

He breathed deeply. "I hope so."

"If you think it's safe to move, I think the comms station is the third or fourth room on the right," she whispered, trying to recall the schematic Al had shown her.

He let go of her hand to grope along the wall, and she followed closely behind, counting the doorways they passed.

"This is three." He pushed open a door and faint, yellow lights flickered on.

Bridget blinked a few times as her eyes adjusted. "This looks like something."

The room wasn't large, but held a wall of monitors and a few consoles with lots of buttons and keyboards. Kax sat down on one of the rolling chairs and began flipping switches.

"Do you know how to work this?" she asked as she watched him.

"I've seen a system like this before. It's pretty basic, which makes sense for a mining colony that hasn't been operational in years."

"So I take it you're used to sneaking into places?"

He kept his eyes on the console. "It isn't my first time. I'm just glad it all came back to me."

"I guess it's like riding a bike?"

He looked up, his brows creased together.

"No bikes on the Drexian home world, either?"

"Sorry," he said. "What is a bike?"

She waved a hand in the air. "Never mind. It means something you never forget how to do once you learn."

The corner of his mouth curved up. "I suppose intelligence work is like these bikes of yours then."

"So this isn't a one-off? You're really going back to being a spy full time?" For some reason the thought of Kax going on intelligence missions made her stomach clench.

"If I can get you back in one piece."

Bridget felt a burst of irritation. "So saving me is like your audition?"

He angled his head at her, his green eyes holding hers. "I wouldn't put it that way."

Static crackled as a blurred image appeared on the active monitor, and then Dorn's face came into view. "Kax! Brother, we thought we'd lost you. You didn't make the rendezvous point or contact us on the agreed channel."

Kax dragged a hand through his hair and his shoulders dropped a few inches. “Dorn.” He exhaled and leaned forward on one elbow. “We got hit during the jump and had to make a pit stop.”

“We?” Dorn said. “Does that mean you found her?”

“Affirmative,” Kax said. “The bride is with me, and is unharmed.”

Unharmed maybe, thought Bridget, but pretty pissed at being called “the bride.”

“‘The bride’ has a name,” she said, leaning close to Kax so she could be seen on Dorn’s monitor.

“Bridget!” Mandy’s face appeared next to Dorn’s. “I’m so relieved to see you.”

Bridget couldn’t help smiling at the woman, and some of her irritation at the bonehead Drexians melted away. “Me too, girl. I can’t wait to get back to the station and toss back few of those Tiki bar cocktails with you.”

She saw Dorn scowl and mutter something, and Mandy elbowed him and giggled.

“Tell your overprotective hubby he’s welcome to join us, if he doesn’t mind listening to girl talk,” Bridget said, smiling at her friend’s obvious happiness and perching on Kax’s lap so she wouldn’t have to bend over uncomfortably to get her head visible in the inset screen.

Dorn said something else, and Mandy’s face became serious. “Where are you two anyway?”

Kax shifted underneath her, and Bridget became aware of exactly where she was sitting. She stood and moved a few steps away, feeling her cheeks flush despite her decision not to let Kax affect her anymore.

Kax leaned closer to the monitor. “We’re at an abandoned mining colony in the Quantrax system.”

Mandy disappeared from the screen as Dorn’s face filled it.

"It's Validian," Bridget added, speaking loudly enough so Dorn could hear her.

Kax gave her a curious look, but continued. "Bridget says it was originally Validian. The Kronock destroyed this place and left sentries as guards."

Dorn's brows pressed together into a single line. "The Kronock are there?"

"A rudimentary, robotic version," Kax told him. "More machine than the fighters we engaged."

"More technology we weren't aware of." Dorn rubbed a hand over his face. "How soon can you get out of there?"

"We're down to one engine, so I either have to try to fix it, or see how lucky I feel flying on half power through Kronock space." He leaned closer to the monitor. "Brother, the Kronock are using this abandoned colony to store radioactive material."

"*Grek*," Dorn said. "Okay, first we need to get you both out of there, then we can worry about what the Kronock are using that for. We've honed in on your signal, so I'm going to—"

His voice cut out as the monitor went dead, and the power spluttered before dying completely and leaving them in darkness.

CHAPTER SIXTEEN

For a moment, Kax was grateful for the darkness. At least Bridget wouldn't see the bulge he'd been trying to hide since she sat on his lap.

"Not this again," Bridget said, her words dying out as they both heard the outside door open and the thud of heavy footsteps.

He stood and closed the distance between himself and Bridget, feeling for her in the darkness and grasping her hand, holding the blaster tightly in his other. The movements were not those of the robot sentries, but he doubted they were friends, either. Not if they'd killed the power in the building.

No. Whoever it was knew they were inside and wanted to get them at a disadvantage. As Kax tried to see anything through the inky blackness, he considered their options. Make a run for it through the building in the dark, or stay in the room and hide, hoping the intruder didn't find them or didn't look hard. Even though he felt Bridget's hand trembling in his, he knew they couldn't stay there and wait to be picked off.

Better to make a run for it and fight their way out if they had to.

He tugged her hand and she followed him as he felt his way silently to the doorway and into the hall, heading away from the door leading outside. He tucked her behind him as he backed down the hall holding the blaster in one outstretched arm, even though he could see nothing.

"You can't escape me." The voice reverberated through the corridor, and he felt Bridget jump and then move closer to him.

It was Krav, the Kronock who'd taken Bridget out from under his nose and seemed to think he could take her again. Kax tightened his grip on her hand, partly to reassure her and partly to reassure himself. He flipped up his hood and pulled hers up over her face.

No way was he letting that monster take her. He'd seen the way the Kronock looked at her, and now he knew what he wanted from her. Kax knew without a doubt he'd die before letting her be taken again. He moved faster, backing her down the hall and hoping there was another way out. The footsteps clomped closer, and he wondered if the Kronock could see them in the dark. He wouldn't be surprised, considering how they'd clearly been augmenting themselves.

"She is mine." The voice grew louder.

Kax heard the sound of a door opening and light entered the building from the opposite end. Another door, he thought, as the outside haze illuminated the twisted face of the commanding alien advancing on them. Kax spun around to see a pair of Kronock fighters entering from the second exit, and he fired on them as he ran forward, with Bridget close on his heels.

The fighters were startled and fell back through the doorway, as blaster fire hit them square in the chest. Kax didn't slow down, leaping over them and turning to see Bridget do the same much more gracefully than him, her legs almost becoming parallel to the ground. The Kronock chasing them ran as well, his heavy legs causing the floor to shake as he pounded closer.

They ran outside into the choking, swirling air. He squinted, trying to see through the glowing red haze.

"The ship," Kax cried, the words muffled in his suit.

They ran fast along the side of the building, Kax looking over his shoulder but not seeing the dark, hulking Kronock behind them. They passed the first building, and Kax saw blinking dots of light ahead. He fired at them but didn't slow, hearing the sentries hit the ground but not able to see them through the storm.

He kept running, holding tight to Bridget's hand and hoping his sense of direction was taking him toward their ship. He felt her stumble behind him, but he pulled her up before she hit the ground. He could hear the clomping of feet behind them and feel the ground trembling. Blaster fire erupted in front of him and Kax dodged to the side, pulling Bridget closer. He couldn't see who was firing, but he could feel the heat of the blasts as they skimmed his shoulder.

The oxygen in his mask had started to run low, no doubt due to how heavily he was sucking in breath. It made his head ache and his legs feel heavy. He felt Bridget's hand slipping from his as her pace also slowed. He gave his head a firm shake. This was not the time to let up. They had to make it to the ship. He clutched her hand and powered forward.

As they approached where he was sure he'd landed the shuttle, Kax slammed on the brakes. The massive Krav stepped out in front of him, barring the way. Kax felt Bridget bump into him then heard her gasp as she registered the dark outline of the enemy commander. How had he gotten in front of them?

Kax sucked in air, his vision blurring. Had they been running in circles?

He turned to run back the way they'd come, but a line of fighters materialized behind them, their bulky outlines glinting through the dense air. He could tell these weren't the sentries, but were the fast-moving Kronock fighters who'd only been slightly altered.

Bridget clung to his arm, and he felt her gasping for breath. His stomach clenched as he once again did a mental run-down of his options, which were shrinking by the minute.

"If you surrender yourself to me, I will let the Drexian live."

Kax could barely see the Kronock's face, but he could hear the self-satisfied victory in his voice.

"Otherwise, I will cut him down in front of you. Your choice." The Kronock fighters raised their weapons in unison and aimed them at him. He could see the red glow of dozens of laser gun sights bouncing across his body.

Bridget inhaled sharply beside him, and he felt her hand slip out of his.

"No." He reached for her. "You can't do this."

"I can't bear to see them kill you." Her voice was small behind the clear window of the environmental suit and through the howling wind, even though he knew she was screaming to be heard. "This way, there's still a chance you can come for me again."

He watched as she took small steps toward the huge Kronock, glancing back over her shoulder at him. His heart constricted as he saw the fear in her wide eyes. He knew he might never get her back once the Kronock commander had her again, and he was sure they wouldn't let him live, no matter what empty promises they made. Even as his head throbbed from lack of oxygen, he tried to think of solutions while panic and despair threatened to overtake him. There was no way out. Not with both of them alive.

Maybe his brother had been right. Maybe he'd been wrong to take this mission. He thought about Dorn and felt glad his brother had found happiness. If that was all he left behind, it was enough for him. Thinking of Dorn made something in his brain snap into place. What would his brother do? Something unexpected, for sure, and probably dangerous. Something they'd never expect.

He fisted his free hand into a steely ball. Even if it meant death, he was not going to let Bridget be taken. Before she was within the enemy's reach, he clicked a setting on his blaster and shot her in the back.

The woman slumped to the ground, and he darted forward and scooped her up, hearing the Kronock leader bellow at his soldiers to hold their fire. Cursing as he ran, he dodged the bigger and slower-moving Kronock commander and jabbed at his own wrist controller.

"This had better work," he muttered to himself, as the door to the shuttle opened and he ran on board, dropping Bridget's body to the floor and pressing his controller to close the door behind him.

He could see the Kronock soldiers running toward him and shooting as he powered up the shuttle and pressed a sequence of commands into the console. Through the fiery, swirling winds, he spotted the commander waving soldiers to their ships, as his shuttle hovered a few feet off the ground before taking off. He punched the final button, then picked up Bridget and ran to the back of the shuttle, kicking at the release for the back hatch and watching as the short ramp dropped down. He pulled her tight to his chest as he dropped out of the hatch and hit the ground in a crouch, stumbling forward and righting himself before pressing his wrist control and sending the shuttle rocketing up into the sky.

He ran as fast as he could away from the buildings and the Kronock ships lifting off the ground to follow his shuttle. Cresting a small hill, he dropped down so he and Bridget were out of sight, and braced himself for what he knew was coming.

An explosion lit up the sky above them, and Kax knew it had worked. His shuttle had self-destructed just as he'd programmed it to do. He let out a breath and sank down, curling his body over Bridget's limp one, in case there was any fallout.

There was more screaming on the ground as the Kronock forces clearly tried to determine what had happened.

"Who fired on that ship?" the Kronock commander bellowed. When none of his soldiers answered him, his rage-filled scream tore through the air.

The voices weren't far from where Kax lay with Bridget. He held his breath, betting on the thick atmosphere and general chaos to keep them from being discovered.

"Return to Choor Dar," the Kronock yelled to his troops as he stalked past them only meters away then dropped his voice to a menacing growl. "I will have to find another human."

Kax felt the small, unmoving woman beneath him and hoped his gamble had paid off.

CHAPTER SEVENTEEN

Bridget heard the scream and felt the wind beating against her. She tried to open her eyes but the red haze blinded her, so she raised a hand to cover them. She felt her body being rolled underneath something and Kax pressing up against her as the stone overhang she was looking up at shielded them from some of the elements.

"Don't move," the voice was soft and right in her ear. "I don't want them to see us."

It took her a while to piece together where she was and what was happening. The last thing she remembered was walking toward the scary Kronock and feeling a blinding pain in her back. After that, everything had gone dark. Kax. She felt a moment of panic he'd been shot, too, but then realized it was his voice in her ear and his body shielding her from the worst of the storm. Bridget tried to take a deep breath, but inhaling only made her head ache more.

She instinctively took the front of Kax's shirt in her fists and pulled him closer until his face was burrowed in her neck and she felt the hard planes of his chest press against her breasts.

"You okay?" his words were choked and barely audible through their face masks.

She moved her head up and down, hearing nothing but the roar of ship engines blasting off close enough to feel the heat of their exhaust. When the ground stopped trembling and the engine noise had grown faint, they lay breathing together for a few moments, his chest rising and falling along with hers.

Kax moved out from under the rock and pulled her out, as well. They stood side by side, peering through the opaque air.

"It worked." He sounded surprised as he wrapped an arm around her. "They're gone."

Bridget recognized the faint outline of the buildings and attempted to locate their shuttle. "Where's our ship?" Her legs buckled and he swung her up into his arms, hurrying back to the nearest building.

Normally, Bridget would have complained bitterly about a man carrying her, but since her legs felt like jelly and her chest ached, she let him carry on without saying a word.

He tugged at the door and she pointed to the fallen Kronock lying at their feet, motioning at Kax to press the hand to the door panel. Kax raised an eyebrow, but followed her direction. Once inside, he slammed the door behind them and stepped over the broken bodies of the Kronock robots, cradling her even closer. He pulled off his face mask, gasping for breath, before doing the same to hers.

"I can walk, you know." She let her head rest on his chest while she argued. It felt good to breathe in regular air, even if the old barracks smelled musty and she knew she was inhaling as much dust as anything.

"You've been shot." He continued down the hall until they reached the sick bay and he pushed open the swinging doors.

Bridget shielded her eyes from the bright lights flickering on, but grinned as Kax placed her gently on the bed. “Hey Al, I’m back.”

No response.

She looked up at the ceiling and the various arms and wands extending down. “Hello? Doctor?”

A series of lights flashed above her. “Hello, Brid-get. Welcome back.”

“She’s been shot with a blaster,” Kax said, the impatience clear in his voice.

The curved bar lowered and began scanning her, stopping at her neck. “Please remove all extraneous fabric, Bridget.”

“This again.” She sighed and pulled off her environmental suit then untied the drawstring at her waist, pulling her legs up so she could slip out of the baggy pants.

Kax looked down at the floor then turned to face away from her. “Do you need help?” he asked over his shoulder.

“I got it,” she said. “Trust me. It’s easier for me to undress myself than for you to try to.”

He cleared his throat and shifted from one foot to the other as she pulled the T-shirt over her head and lay back on the platform completely naked.

“All right, Al. Do your worst.”

The scan began again with the blue light running the length of her body. “I do not think you wish me to ‘do my worst,’ Bridget.”

“It’s an expression, Al.” She allowed herself a small laugh. “I know you’re incapable of doing a bad job.”

“That is correct. I have the accumulated knowledge of thousands of years of medical training in order to provide the most accurate diagnosis.”

“Didn’t I tell you he was a charmer?” she said to Kax.

"How is she?" Kax didn't turn his head. "Did she sustain damage from the blaster?"

The curved bar lifted into the ceiling and a wand dropped with a single, small needle that pricked the side of Bridget's arm before she could think to protest.

"Minimal damage," Al said in his robotic voice. "Her heart and lungs have above average capacity for organic creatures of her size, so the blaster fire did no permanent damage. I have administered a healing agent to speed her recovery."

Kax's shoulders sagged. "Thank the gods. What about exposure to radiation?"

"Negative," Al said.

Kax let out a long breath.

"How many times do I have to tell you?" Bridget said. "I'm tougher than I look. It's going to take more than being stunned by a Kronock blaster to bring me down."

"This wound was not created by a Kronock weapon," Al said. "The heat signature in your body is very different from the one in your friend when he was wounded by the Kronock, and in the Validians when I treated them from Kronock blaster wounds."

Bridget propped herself up on her elbows. "If the Kronock didn't shoot me, then who did?"

Kax started to turn, caught a glimpse of her still naked body and stopped. "I did, but only—"

"You shot me?" Bridget cut him off. "Why? I mean I know you don't really like me, but did you really have to shoot me?"

His hands became fists. "I did it to save you. It was my last resort, since you stupidly decided to give yourself up to the Kronock."

"Stupid?" She sat up all the way. "I was trying to save your sorry ass from being blown away by about a hundred Kronock."

"It isn't your job to save me." His voice was a low growl. "It's my job to rescue you. Not the other way around."

"Well, tough." She swung her legs over the side of the platform and glared at his back. "You may not care much about me, but I care about you, and there was no way I was going to watch you die if I could save you."

"Please lie down, Brid-get," Al's stilted voice cut through the fighting. "Your heart rate is rising."

"You think I don't care about you?" Kax asked.

"Oh, I know you care about the mission and getting me back to the station." Bridget's voice sounded shrill even to her own ears. "But I've seen the way you pull away from me and flinch when I touch you. It's clear I'm nothing more than the mission to you." Her voice cracked. "You won't even look at me now."

"That's because I'm afraid if I look at you, I'm going to throw you down on that table and take you right here."

Bridget felt like all the fight had been knocked out of her. "What?"

"I've been battling it, but I don't know how much longer I can hold out." His breathing was ragged. "Please put on your clothes, Bridget."

As she looked at his broad back, the muscles bunched so that the raised bumps down his spine pressed hard against the snug fabric of the environmental suit, she imagined running her hands over them and her nipples hardened. As much as she didn't want to fall for anyone, she couldn't deny he stirred something in her no one had in a long time. Ignoring her feelings hadn't worked, but maybe burning them off another way would. "No."

"Bridget." His voice was pleading with her as he put his hands to his head.

"I don't care about your mission, or the Drexian rules, or

any other Drexian warrior. I want you." She hitched in her breath. "And right now, I want you inside me, Kax."

With a guttural growl, he turned and advanced on her, his eyes burning as he crushed his mouth to hers. She raked her fingers through his hair as his tongue found hers. There was nothing timid about his kiss as the force of it pushed her back. He claimed her with his mouth as she pulled him deeper to her, wrapping her naked legs around him.

She did believe in lust, after all.

CHAPTER EIGHTEEN

Kax moaned as Bridget used her bare legs to jerk him toward her until his cock pressed against her through his pants. She tilted her hips up to grind against him, and he nearly lost control. She was kissing him like she couldn't get enough of him—her tongue insistent as it stroked his. His brain tried to slow him down, but her raw desire overpowered him, and he lost the internal battle he'd been fighting for days.

"We shouldn't," he said, pulling away for a moment before he pulled her closer.

"Oh, we definitely should." Her words were a series of breathless gasps she whispered into his ear, sending tremors down his spine and causing his nodes to harden. "Unless you have some sexually transmitted disease you need to tell me about."

He shook his head, and she nipped his ear. "Didn't think so. Me, either."

Kax barely registered what she was talking about, as raw desire tore through him. She bit his ear again, this time hard enough to hurt. He growled, low and rough, the sound echoing through his body.

He wanted to be gentle, but he couldn't be. He wanted her too much to take his time, not when she was ripe and ready, her naked body moving against his. He moved his hands to her bare ass and rocked her toward him, his fingers biting into her soft round cheeks.

"I can't go slow," he said. "I need to take you hard."

She nipped his neck. "I want it hard, Kax." She arched her spine and dropped her head back, still holding on to his shoulders. "Make me scream."

His eyes nearly rolled into the back of his head as he drank in the sight of her quivering breasts. He wanted to feel her pleasure first, watch her lose control. He growled as he lowered his head to take one hard nipple inside his mouth.

She cried out, clawing at his back as he teased and sucked her. He moved to the other nipple, lapping at it until she was panting, her breath shallow. She dropped her hands back to the table and leaned back on them, letting her head fall as she moaned and writhed. He looked up and watched the pleasure on her face as she bit down on her bottom lip.

Kax pulled away and ran one hand down her belly, stopping when he reached her narrow strip of dark curls. "Watch me," he said.

She gasped as he rubbed his thumb over her clit, circling it as she quivered in response. "You're making me so wet for you."

"Just the way I like it." He slipped his finger between her slick thighs and worked it inside her. "So ready for me."

Her muscles clenched his finger, making his cock throb as he moved it in and out of her wet heat. "I'm close," she said, her words escaping between sighs.

"Not yet." He crouched between her legs, keeping his finger

inside her, and dragged his tongue between her folds and flicked it over her clit. He moaned. She tasted so good. Sweet and slick. He couldn't imagine ever tiring of licking her soft folds. Not when she bucked and moaned so prettily beneath his hot mouth.

"I can't hold back," she said, the words little more than a gasp.

He slowed his fingers as he swirled his tongue languidly then looked up at her. "I want to be inside you. I want to feel you come."

She nodded, her eyes closed. "I want you inside me."

He straightened up and pulled off his suit, then undid his pants with one hand, letting them drop to the floor while Bridget tugged his shirt over his head and ran her hands down his chest. Her eyes widened when she saw his cock, thick and hard and ready for her. She licked her lips and smiled as she wrapped one hand around his shaft. Gods, the woman drove him crazy.

He pushed her knees back and opened them, gazing down at her hungrily as he dragged his thick head up through her folds, her juices glistening as they covered his swollen crown.

"I need you to take me hard," she said, her eyes half-lidded with desire.

He couldn't pace himself any longer. Kax thrust into her, feeling his cock stretch her, and hearing her suck in air. She was so hot and tight, like a fist squeezing him. He swallowed a cry as he stroked deeper, clutching her hips and pulling her to him.

"So tight," he said, as he bent and buried his head in her neck, inhaling her scent and feeling her skin against his as he lodged himself deep. His body thrummed with a million sensations at once as he dragged himself back out of her, feeling every exquisite jolt as she ran her hands down his back, stroking his nodes.

He pulled back as she lifted one hand and raked it through her hair, her eyes not leaving his as he drove in again and again, her gasps becoming screams. He scooped his hands under her back without pausing his rhythm, lowering his mouth to her neck and feeling her hands on his shoulders, her nails scoring his skin.

"Harder," she begged. "I want it harder."

Pleasure barreled through him as he felt her body begin to ripple, and her husky moans became cries. He pumped faster as she reared up, throwing her head back and screaming as her muscles clamped around his cock, and she spasmed in his arms. Feeling her clench around him made Kax lose all control. He slammed into her, coming in a furious rush of heat as he let out his own roar and emptied inside her.

Bridget trembled as she held on to his slick shoulders, her head resting on his chest. He felt his heart pounding and her own pulse fluttering as he took one of her hands and kissed her palm.

"Is that your way of apologizing for shooting me?" she asked.

He laughed. "Did it work?"

"It's a start." She raised her head and grinned up at him. "I might need a few more apologies before I can truly forgive you, though."

He brushed a strand of hair off her brow. "I live to serve."

"As long as you're only serving me, tough guy."

He put a finger under her chin and tilted her head back, brushing a kiss softly across her lips. "There's only you."

CHAPTER NINETEEN

Bridget held on to him, loving the feel of his bunched up muscles twitching beneath her fingers and the warmth of his skin slick with sweat. She ran her hands down his back, feeling the hard, hot bumps along his spine.

Kax groaned. "Wondering what those are?"

"Nodes," Bridget said. "I've heard the other tributes talking about them. I didn't expect them to be so... firm."

"They aren't always hard," Kax said, trying to catch his breath.

"Oh," Bridget smiled, circling one with the tip of her finger and feeling his body tense. "I like them."

"Your heart rates are alarming," Al's halting voice announced from overhead. "I recommend an injection to bring them back to normal."

A metal swing arm dropped down, and Bridget scooted away from it. "No more needles. We're fine, Al."

"If you say so, Brid-get. I should probably monitor you until your respiration is within accepted norms."

"That sounds like fun," Kax said under his breath.

Bridget tried to give him a severe look but failed, holding a hand over her mouth to keep from giggling. "I promise I'm fine." She met Kax's eyes. "Better than fine actually."

"What about your Drexian?" Al asked. "I report abnormal blood flow and muscle spasms in the legs and buttocks."

Kax shook his head as he tilted his head up. "I guess there's no keeping secrets from you, Al."

"I can help with that, you know." Bridget cocked an eyebrow and slid her hands down to caress his ass.

Kax groaned, leaning his forehead against hers. "Only if you want to give Al more reason to worry."

Bridget slapped one cheek. "As much fun as it is to get post-sex commentary, I think we should find a more appropriate place."

Kax nodded, the heat fading from his eyes. "We can't assume all the Kronock are gone. There could be more sentries, or the others could return, if they figure out I blew up an empty ship."

Bridget shivered a little at the thought of the Kronock leader coming back for her.

Kax pulled her close to him, tucking her head under his chin. "Don't worry. I promised I wouldn't let them take you. That hasn't changed."

Bridget inhaled the warm, masculine scent of his skin and believed him. It had been a long time since she'd felt safe with someone, felt she could trust another person. She felt so secure wrapped in his arms she couldn't imagine leaving. A little part of her was glad they had no way off the colony if it meant being alone with him for longer.

"I don't suppose you located a shower when Al was showing you the colony's schematics?" Kax asked.

"A shower?" Her gaze dropped to their naked, sweaty bodies. "Yeah, that might not be a bad idea. Hey, Al—"

"There is a decontamination shower at the end of the hall, next to the communal bathroom servicing the barracks." Al whirred for a moment. "A private bathroom is located next to the manager's quarters on the upper level."

"Thanks, Al." Kax swung Bridget off the table and into his arms, scooping up their clothes and his blaster with his free arm.

"Please return for a medical assessment if you experience abnormal heart palpitations or irregular breathing."

"Not a chance," Kax muttered.

Bridget elbowed him. "You got it, Al. Thanks for fixing me up."

"You are welcome, Brid-get. Please try to avoid getting shot in the future. It is very detrimental to your health."

"You hear that?" she told Kax, who rolled his eyes.

He strode out of the sick bay and swept the hallway before starting up the stairs, which he took two at a time despite carrying Bridget. She was used to being lifted by male dancers, but their touch had always been part of the performance, and none of the sinewy male dancers she'd worked with had been anything more than friends. Half of them hadn't even played for her team. Being held by Kax, whose wide chest and thick arms dwarfed her, made her feel like nothing in the world could harm her.

"You know I can walk," she said, once they'd reached the top level.

"I know." He didn't put her down, waiting until he'd located the bathroom attached to the manager's room where they'd slept earlier.

Bridget took in the simple, white-tiled room. Aside from the toilet and standing sink, the walk-in shower with glass doors took up most of the space. An empty metal towel rack extended across one wall, and a dried up bar of soap perched on the sink.

Kax flicked the knob in the shower and water spluttered out of the ceiling. He wrenched the soap from the sink and stepped into the shower, pulling Bridget with him.

She gasped as the cool water hit her skin, pressing herself close to him to retain some of his body heat. "I'm guessing this joint doesn't have hot water."

"I'll keep you warm," he said as he rubbed the bar of soap briskly between his hands to create a lather. He stroked his sudsy hands down the length of her body and, despite the cold water, she felt her muscles relaxing under his touch. The soap smelled spicy, with a hint of musk—no surprise if the colony's manager had been a male—but Bridget liked the scent of it on her skin.

She took the soap from Kax and started to return the favor, running her palms down his chest and across his back. She reached down and cupped her hands around his cock, soaping the length of him and feeling him harden in response to her touch.

Bridget knelt down as she let her hands continue down his legs, washing his muscular thighs and calves and letting the water rinse off the soap, sending it spiraling down the drain. Still kneeling, she fisted his cock and ran her tongue over the tip. Kax braced both hands against the shower wall and let out a guttural sound.

Bridget took the head into her mouth, swirling her tongue around it then leaning forward to suck the length of it in. She heard Kax's sharp intake of breath, and felt his muscles tense as she gripped his legs for balance. Moving her mouth up and down his shaft, she sucked him until she felt his cock begin to pulse.

He placed his hands at the back of her head, fisting her hair and pulling her closer, his eyes locked on her as she sucked him deep. "Your lips look so pretty stretched around my cock."

She made a noise in the back of her throat that vibrated in her mouth. He groaned, and she hummed some more, loving the taste of him and the feel of his hardness filling her mouth.

Kax reached down and pulled her up by the arms, flipping her around so she faced away from him and grasping her by the hips. He tilted her ass up and plunged into her with a single hard stroke. Bridget's cries were swallowed by the sound of the water as she flattened her hands against the glass walls, his thick cock lodged deep inside her. She loved feeling him fill her completely, and felt a searing bolt of heat as he dragged himself out and thrust back inside.

"Feels so good," she said, the words escaping between jagged breaths.

His steady strokes made her arch her back and open her legs wider for him, lifting her ass and leaning lower so he could power deeper. She loved the feeling of being split as he buried his cock inside her again and again. Kax reached a hand around and found her swollen clit, circling it slowly with one finger. It was almost too much, and she rocked her hips into him, feeling the surges of pleasures begin to course through her body.

"Come for me, beautiful," Kax said, his voice husky. "I want to feel you milk my cock."

His words drove her over the edge. Bridget felt her body buck against him, but he held her hips tight, ramming his cock to the hilt as she splintered apart, screaming his name, her body clenching him again and again. His cries joined hers as he pistoned faster, throwing his head back and emptying himself while clutching her hips tightly.

Bridget slumped against the shower wall, her legs weak and shaky. She was vaguely aware of the water pouring over them—which had gone from cool to cold—but her scorched body didn't mind.

Kax looped a hand around her waist to keep her from falling, even though she felt his own legs quivering. He kissed her neck and ran one hand up to cup her breast, even his soft touch making her twitch in response. Reaching behind him, he turned off the water.

Bridget faced him and wrapped her arms around his neck. "That was officially the best shower I've ever had."

He captured the side of her face in one hand and lowered his mouth to hers, his tongue parting her lips gently and his kiss soft, but searching. When he pulled back, his eyes seemed to be memorizing her face. Even in her euphoric daze, his expression made her worry.

CHAPTER TWENTY

Kax stared up at the ceiling while Bridget slept beside him, a thin sheet pulled over both their bodies. They'd come out of the shower dripping wet and crawled into the big bed, locking the door and pushing the standing dresser in front of it. It might not stop a blaster, but it would slow down intruders.

After they'd shared a couple of the remaining ration pouches and chugged some water, Bridget had curled up with one arm draped over his chest and dropped off to sleep. He hadn't been so lucky. Even though the room was dark and quiet, his mind raced. He replayed the image of Bridget falling after he'd shot her and then the contrasting image of her with his cock buried inside her. Kax gave an abrupt shake of his head.

Stop it, he told himself. *You're fooling yourself. She was never meant to be yours.*

He tugged her closer, loving the feel of her soft cheek resting on his chest muscle and of her warm breath on his skin. Then why did this feel so right? Why did she feel like his?

It didn't matter what he felt. What mattered was his duty to his people. His father had drilled that into him since he was a child. Nothing was more important than serving the Drexian empire, and living up to his family name. He could almost hear his father's words echoing in his head.

Kax looked down at the black hair splayed across his chest. He knew he had no right to Bridget. She was a tribute bride who had been meant for another, and now would be matched to a worthy, virile warrior. He was neither of those things. He was damaged.

His chest tightened as he thought back to the intelligence mission where he'd unknowingly exposed himself to radiation. He'd ended up saving thousands of lives, but a part of him wished he'd never gone. A small, selfish part wished he'd never disabled the weapons and ruined his chances of ever taking a mate.

He blew out a long breath. It was pointless to think about it. The damage was done. No female would want a man they knew would never be able to give them children. Even if they did, the Drexian leadership would never allow it. Females were too valuable to waste on a Drexian who could never help the species continue.

Kax was only happy his father wasn't alive to witness his shame. He could imagine the words he'd have for a man who couldn't do his duty. It had always been impressed upon Kax that as the eldest, it was up to him to carry on the family name and further solidify the reputation of one of the most notable Drexian houses. Now that responsibility fell to his younger brother, Dorn, who had taken a mate and would take Kax's place on the High Command.

Kax didn't regret leaving High Command, or going back to the nomad's life of military intelligence. What he already regretted was leaving Bridget. He traced a finger absently on her back, enjoying the feel of her smooth skin. Leaning his head down, he breathed in the smell of her—soap from the shower and something sweeter, a scent that was distinctly her. He would miss how she felt, how she smelled, how she tasted. He inhaled again, trying to commit her scent to memory.

She shifted in her sleep, stretching one hand up to touch the stubble of his cheek. Even the brush of her fingertips on his face felt electric, sending a jolt all the way to his toes and making his cock jerk to life.

He frowned at himself. He knew he needed to put some distance between them, but when it came to her, his body betrayed him. All the discipline he'd cultivated as an warrior flew out the window the moment she twitched her ass at him. And what a nice ass it was.

He let his hand drift down and palm one high, rounded cheek. She let out a breathy moan and moved her hips so his hand slipped down between her legs to where she was hot and wet. He pressed his eyes shut and tried to ignore the rush of blood to his cock as his fingers slipped inside her slick folds. Another throaty noise from Bridget made him pull his hand back, cursing himself for his weakness.

He opened his eyes and she was staring up at him, her gaze molten. "Don't stop, tough guy."

"This isn't right," he said. "We shouldn't be together."

"Why not?" She pushed herself up so the sheet slid off her back. "I know now I don't repulse you."

He tried to keep his eyes from drifting from her face to her bare breasts. Far from repulsing him, the sight of her made every other thought leave his mind. He shook his head.

"Listen, I don't know how things work with Drexians, but on Earth the women get a say in who they hook up with or marry. A big say." She put a delicate hand on his chest. "I pick you."

He closed a hand over hers. "You don't know everything about me."

"I know enough. You're brave, you're kind, and you're amazing in bed." She shrugged. "What else is there?"

A family, he thought. A legacy, a lineage, a name that would continue. Even if she didn't care about those things, his people did.

Another shake of his head. "I can't. It's impossible."

Her eyes flashed and she snatched her hand back. "Can't or won't? What? Does having a mate interfere with your big plans of being a spy again? Do you think I'd cramp your style? Or maybe you want to be free to fuck anyone you want?"

He felt stung by her words and felt his own heat rising. "That's not it. I don't want to fuck anyone else."

"You sure you don't want to keep your options open when you hit the brothels at the alien outposts, or the pleasure planets?"

He opened and closed his mouth. "How do you know about those?"

She shrugged. "People on the space station talk, and I'm a good listener. I know all about how Drexians learn their tricks before being matched up with a tribute bride."

Kax had been to the pleasure planets—every Drexian warrior had—but they'd given him nothing compared to what Bridget had. "I have no desire to be with anyone else, but I can't be with you, either. It's out of my hands."

She glared at him. "What does that even mean?"

He wanted to tell her, but the shame of admitting he was less than a man made the words choke in his throat. How could he tell her he could never fill her belly with a child, could never give her a family, and could never be a father? He gave an abrupt shake of his head.

"Aren't tribute brides the Drexians' most valuable asset?" Bridget asked.

"Yes, but—"

"And aren't you supposed to give me anything I want? Isn't that the whole purpose of your fancy space station? To keep us pampered and spoiled so we'll be happy enough to help you keep your species going?" She didn't wait for him to reply. "Then I want you. That's what will make me happy. I want you in my bed every night, fucking my brains out."

Heat coursed through him. It was all he wanted, too. He took her face in his hand and stroked his thumb across her cheek, feeling his resolve weaken. "You're sure you want me? You're sure you want this? Even if..." He paused.

"No matter what," she said, her eyes meeting his with equal fire as she moved her head to take his thumb into her mouth.

"You don't know what you're saying," he insisted, his eyes fluttering shut as she sucked his thumb hard.

She reached down and clasped a hand around his cock, her fingertips not quite meeting, and he released her face, his eyes snapping open.

"I know what I want," she said. "I may not believe in fairy-tales or soul mates, or any of that crap, but I know I've never had this kind of chemistry with anyone. I know you make me feel safe."

He flipped her onto her back as white-hot desire surged through him. He crushed his mouth to hers, devouring the sweet taste of her as he kissed her deeply. Bridget's hungry noises made his blood ignite. His tongue swirled with hers, his own sounds becoming husky when her fingers caressed his nodes, stroking them to hardness. He reared back and grasped one ankle in each hand. "This is what you want?"

She nodded, her nipples tightening into hard points.

He opened her legs until she was spread wide for him, and he gazed hungrily at her. She moaned and bit the edge of her bottom lip. He pushed the crown of his cock inside her and watched her pupils dilate. "You want more?"

"I want all of you," she said.

"You make it so hard for me to go slow," he said, feeling his tightly coiled need igniting.

She ran one finger down her body and teased her own clit. "I like making you lose control."

"You do, do you?" Her words and the sight of her own finger circling her pleasure center made him moan. "I may have to punish you for that, naughty girl."

She licked her lips. "Yes, please."

He surged into her, holding her legs open wide and watching as his thick cock stretched her, claiming her as his. Bridget screamed as he pounded into her, arching her back so he could go deeper.

"You like your punishment?"

"Hurts so good," she gasped.

"That's my naughty girl." Kax didn't stop until he felt her muscles clench his cock like a vise, the spasms rocking her body and making her cry out. The sensations slammed through him—wave after scorching wave—as he climaxed with a final hard stroke and burrowed his cock into her.

Panting, he looked down at her flushed face and the satisfied grin she gave him. He released her ankles and wrapped her legs around his waist, then collapsed next to her.

Bridget rolled on top of him. "If that was your way of talking me out of it, then you're going to need to try harder, tough guy."

Kax ignored the gnawing feeling in his gut as he slid one arm underneath her and pulled her closer.

CHAPTER TWENTY-ONE

Bridget ran through the darkness, her bare feet barely landing on the loamy soil as she dodged trees and tangled with underbrush. Her toes felt cold, so she looked down and saw frost glistening on the ground. The moonlight made it shimmer, and she thought how pretty it was before her brain questioned why there was snow *or* a moon. The mining colony didn't have a moon that she recalled.

Somehow she knew she was on Earth, but that didn't make sense. How had she gotten back to Earth? The last thing she remembered was being with Kax.

She glanced desperately around. Where was he? He wouldn't have left her by herself, would he? The woods seemed empty, aside from her, but that also made no sense. Her head spun as she heard the sound of footsteps in the distance. These weren't soft like hers. They pounded the ground and echoed in her ears, and she began running again. Bridget's heart raced as she ran, and she looked back over her shoulder, seeing nothing but the dark.

Looking ahead, she saw a hand reaching back for her. Bridget reached desperately for the hand. She couldn't tell if it was a man's hand or woman's hand, young or old, she just knew she had to grab it. She was so close, their fingertips were nearly touching. Then she lunged, and the hand dissolved into a swirl of mist.

Bridget bolted upright in bed, her breath heavy. The room was dark, but she wasn't in the woods, and there was no frost on the ground. She snatched her feet up under her to warm them as she tried to calm herself.

"It was just a dream," she whispered to herself, comforted by the sound of her own voice in the stillness.

Kax grunted and rolled over, still deep in sleep.

She didn't want to wake him. Nightmares were par for the course. She'd been having them since she was a child. She was always running—being chased by someone she never saw—she was always alone, and she was never able to reach the hand. It didn't take a shrink to pinpoint her abandonment issues. Not that Bridget had ever gone to a psychiatrist. Her grandmother had raised her with the philosophy that you didn't complain and you soldiered through—no matter what. Life wasn't fair, but it didn't do you any good to dwell on it. That's why they'd almost never talked about her parents' death. The only time she allowed herself to feel fear or doubt was in her dreams. She rubbed her arms briskly.

"Are you okay?" Kax's voice made her jump. He was propped up with his elbows behind him, the sheet down around his waist and exposing his bare chest.

"Of course." She stopped rubbing her arms. "I'm sorry I woke you."

He sat up and pulled her close. "You're shaking."

"It's nothing. A nightmare. I get them all the time."

"You're safe now," he said. "You're with me."

Considering what had happened and where they were, she wasn't sure that was entirely true, but the warmth of his body comforted her. She let herself sag against him. "But you won't always be around. No one ever stays forever."

"I'm not going anywhere."

"I know you don't want to," Bridget said, her voice small. "But people always leave, whether they want to or not. That's why I can't..."

"Can't...?" he prodded, his tone gentle.

She let out a long breath. It was easier to say it in the dark where she couldn't see his reaction. "Why I can't believe in happily ever after, or soul mates, or forever, or any of those things. Love doesn't save you. My parents loved each other, and me, and that didn't save them from being killed in a car crash. My grandmother loved me, but that didn't mean she could prevent herself from dying and leaving me to the foster system. Love made everything hurt more. Life isn't like a fairy-tale. Not the life I've known, at least."

He stroked her arm. "Life isn't always fair."

She gave a brusque shake of her head. "It doesn't matter. Losing people toughened me up. I can survive being alone. I've had to be on my own enough to know I'll always be able to take care of myself."

"I know you're tough," he said, amusement in his voice. "I've seen you fight. I've also seen the side of you that isn't so tough."

She thought of their bodies entwined, and her cheeks warmed. She wanted to insist that it had just been sex, but that would have been a lie. It had been great sex, but it had been more than that.

"Is that what you want?" he asked, his voice soft. "To be alone?"

"What do you want?" she asked, too scared to give him an honest answer. What she really wanted was for him to tell her he loved her and would fight to be with her, and that he'd never leave her. She wanted him to prove her wrong and fill the gaping hole in her heart.

"Something I can never have," he said, his voice thick.

The hopelessness in his voice made her skin go cold. Before she could make him explain, she heard it. A footstep. The heartbeat she'd just calmed began racing again. "Do you hear that?"

He went still. She held her breath while they both listened. Another thud on the floor—not robotic, though. Someone was on the hallway.

"Not machine," he whispered, tensing beside her.

Steady footsteps—from more than one set of feet—grew louder as they got closer. Kax slipped out of bed, pulling his cargo pants on quietly and handing Bridget's clothes to her. She fumbled to get dressed in bed and joined him at the door.

"Do you think the Kronock are back?" she asked, her voice barely audible.

"Doesn't sound like them," he said. "Too hesitant. The Kronock would come in with blasters firing."

He pushed her back with one hand. "I'm going to go out and see. You stay in here."

"Are you nuts? What if it *is* them or someone worse?"

"Then they'll get in here eventually." He pressed his lips to her forehead. "I'd rather take them on my own terms."

She let out a breath. What was it about men that made them always want to run headfirst into battle?

The footsteps had stopped, so Kax pushed the dresser away from the door and opened it with his blaster drawn. The hallway was illuminated by a single emergency light at the far

end, the warm glow making it possible to identify shapes and not much else.

"Drop your weapon." The voice did not belong to Kax, but it was familiar.

"Dorn?" Kax asked. "Brother, is that you?"

A loud sigh. "Am I glad to see you. This is the third floor we've cleared. I was starting to think you and the bride had been taken. Is Bridget still with you?"

"Right here." Bridget stepped out from the room and gave a little wave, trying not to feel irritated at being called "the bride" again.

Dorn stood halfway down the hall, with several other Drexian soldiers. He wore his military uniform, his dark hair shaggy around his ears. He cleared the distance between them in a few long strides, holding a bulky rifle across his body. When he got closer, she noticed the brilliant emerald eyes she'd grown accustomed to in Kax's face.

"There are a lot of people back on the station who're eager to see you," Dorn said, giving her odd attire the once-over and turning his attention to his brother. "And eager to award you commendations."

"Commendations?" Kax lowered his blaster as the Drexian soldiers with Dorn joined them, forming a semicircle behind their commander.

"For rescuing a tribute bride out from under the nose of the enemy." Dorn clapped a hand on his shoulder. "Looks like you haven't lost your touch." His eyes dropped to Kax's bare chest. "Although you seem to have lost your shirt."

Kax ignored the comment and the curious look his brother gave him as he looked between her and him. "Then they'll be even more pleased when we tell them what we know about the Kronock's plans."

Dorn cocked an eyebrow. "Anything that should worry me?"

"They're planning an imminent invasion of Earth. Have been for a while," Kax said. "They didn't take Bridget to get a response from us. They took her so they could use her DNA to create some sort of hybrid human-Kronock."

Dorn's mouth gaped. "What?"

"They didn't get to," Bridget said. "At least I'm pretty sure they didn't, but they said something about making it easier to invade Earth."

Dorn tilted his head at her. "That doesn't make sense. Then again, the Kronock have a lot more tricks up their sleeves than we thought they did. At least you stopped this part of their plan."

Bridget didn't mention that the plan to take her seemed more like a personal mission of Krav's, than anything else. She didn't like thinking he might still be coming for her.

"I hope you have room for us," Kax said, ducking into the room and grabbing both his and Bridget's environmental suits. "I had to blow up the shuttle."

Dorn gave him a look. "I'm assuming you had an excellent reason."

"I thought it was the kind of thing you would do." Kax thumped his brother on the back, then handed Bridget her suit and proceeded to tug his on. "I'd rather not be here when the Kronock figure out I've tricked them, though. At the moment, they believe Bridget and I both died in the explosion. I'd like to keep it that way."

Dorn jerked a thumb toward the exit. "Let's go."

The other soldiers led the way down the hall, laser rifles held up. Kax put a hand on her back as they followed and she liked feeling his warmth, even though his arm wasn't around her.

Dorn glanced over his shoulder. "Her fiancé will be happy to hear we've got her."

Kax's steps faltered. "Fiancé? I thought he died in the battle."

"The first one did, but they've already made a new match. An impressive match. The son of High Commander Terk."

Kax's hand dropped from her back. "So soon?"

"What if I don't want to be matched with this guy?" Bridget asked, her words sharper than she'd intended them to be.

Dorn glanced back at her, one eyebrow cocked. "I thought you were okay with the deal. Mandy told me you were more eager than she was, although that wouldn't have been hard."

It was no secret—even to Dorn—how Mandy had railed against being a tribute bride, until she'd fallen for her fiancé. The problem for Bridget wasn't the concept of the tribute bride system. It was that, despite her insistence in not believing in love, she'd fallen for Kax.

"Karsh is a decent warrior," Dorn said. "Not as much of a pretty boy as my brother here, but you can't have everything."

Kax didn't look at her. "You should give him a chance."

Bridget was glad the other Drexians were facing forward so they couldn't see her shoot daggers at him. How could he suggest she seriously consider another mate when they'd just rolled out of bed together? She was still sore from him being insider her, and he was fine with this Karsh guy marrying her? She'd spilled her guts to him, and he turned around and told her to accept a match with another warrior?

Her cheeks burned with humiliation. What was going on? Only hours ago he'd seemed convinced by her arguments. Then again, should she really have to convince him they should be together? She knew she didn't understand Drexian culture, but his reluctance made no sense to her. If anyone deserved to be awarded a tribute bride, it should be Kax. He was a member of the elite ruling class, and now he'd pulled off a rescue mission, saving her from the Kronock and relaying secrets about the enemy. He should be able to have his pick of brides, even one who'd already been matched with someone else. Why did he seem so sure it could never happen?

She looked at the rigid set of his face as he walked beside her. He'd given her up so quickly she felt like her head was spinning. Had she read things so wrong? Sure, he was attracted to her. He couldn't pretend he wasn't when her lightest touch made him hard, but she saw now it wasn't enough. What she'd thought was something deeper, he must not have. Otherwise, he'd fight for her. Tell the High Command to go fuck themselves and claim Bridget for himself. Maybe to Kax it was just sex. Great, bone-melting sex, but nothing worth going against the Drexian traditions or rules for.

"You're right," she said. "No reason not to, right?"

Dorn held open the door to the stairwell, letting her pass underneath his arm and falling in line once Kax walked by. "I'll brief you on your next mission once we're aboard."

"Next mission?" Kax asked.

Dorn put a hand on his brother's shoulder. "You can take a day or two for R and R if you need it, but then the High Command wants you to do some recon on the Kronock research facility."

Kax looked straight ahead. "I won't need any time off."

Bridget was glad she was holding the metal handrail because her legs nearly buckled when she heard his toneless response. Not only was he not going to fight for her, he wasn't even going to stick around long enough to say a proper good-bye. She leaned against the cool metal, her hands gripping the rail so tightly she knew without looking that her knuckles were white. She'd been wrong about people before, but never this wrong.

This is what happens when you let someone in, the little voice in her head told her. *You knew better than to trust him. There's no such thing as happily ever after. Not for you.*

She bit her bottom lip until she tasted the metallic tang of blood, and she swallowed it down.

CHAPTER TWENTY-TWO

Kax waited until the shuttle had landed on the space station—the spacecraft jolting as the landing gear slapped the floor of the flight deck—to unclasp his seat restraint. He leaned over to assist Bridget, but she'd already undone hers and stood quickly.

"I've got it," she said, not meeting his eyes.

He pressed his lips together but didn't respond. He couldn't say anything, since his brother sat right next to her.

Dorn stood and pounded a hand on his back. "You officially made it back in one piece, and with Bridget. I'd call your mission a success."

Kax glanced at Bridget, now wearing form-fitting cargo pants and a snug T-shirt, courtesy of Mandy, who'd insisted Dorn bring her clothes to wear on the journey back since Bridget had been abducted in a bridesmaid gown. He didn't know when he'd fallen for her, but she'd gone from just another tribute bride to the woman he couldn't stop thinking about. Maybe it was when he'd watched her fight the Kronock by his side, or maybe it was when she'd opened up about her past, but at some point, the female had worked her way into his heart. His gut clenched as he watched her brush her dark hair back from her face, and he thought about those same delicate fingers tending to his wound and digging into his sweaty flesh.

"Ready to face the High Command?" Dorn asked, ripping him away from his thoughts.

Kax pulled his eyes reluctantly from Bridget. "Right now? I thought I'd. . ."

His words trailed off. What had he thought he'd do? Go with Bridget to her quarters? Try to spend one more hour in her arms before leaving? That wouldn't be fair to her. Or to her new mate. He tasted bile in his throat as he thought about the Drexian she'd been matched with.

Karsh, son of Terk, wasn't someone he knew well, but he'd known his father for years as they'd served on the High Command together. One day, Bridget's mate would sit on the High Command. Kax was only glad he wouldn't be around to see it.

"You have other plans?" Dorn raised an eyebrow. "Better to get it over with. They'll want to know why you blew up a shuttle."

"Of course I don't have other plans." His brother was right. Better to deal with the High Command first, so he could secure his next mission as soon as possible. He saw Bridget flinch, her gaze avoiding him. He desperately wanted to reach out for her. She was so close he could smell the sweet scent of her skin, could imagine the softness of her beneath his fingers as he ran a hand down her bare arm. He closed his eyes for a moment as he inhaled deeply, trying to breathe her in, but when he opened his eyes she'd moved away from him.

He snatched his pack from the floor and followed as the door to the shuttle opened. If he could get her away from Dorn for a moment, he could talk to her and explain. He hesitated. Explain what? What could he possibly say? I'm falling for you, but I can't be with you because I can't give you—or the Drexian Empire—offspring? His face warmed at the thought of revealing his humiliation, and he dropped back. What was the point? It wouldn't make any difference if she knew or not, except she'd probably feel pity for him. He clenched his teeth. He couldn't bear pity.

Bridget hurried down the ramp in front of him, and Mandy rushed up to her, throwing her arms around her friend's neck.

"I knew they'd bring you back," Mandy said when she released her, smiling and swiping away tears. She inspected Bridget, running her hands up her arms. "You look okay, but I should take you to the medical bay just in case."

"I'm fine," Bridget said. "Al fixed me up."

Mandy's gaze narrowed. "I want to hear all about this Al guy, but first let's get you checked out."

"Just go along with it," Dorn said. "You know how she loves to patch people up."

Mandy shot her mate a look, but Bridget could see it was more playful than angry.

"I hope you didn't get into too much trouble without me, girl," Bridget said, falling in step next to Mandy and looping an arm around her waist.

"How could I get in trouble working in the medical bay?" Mandy said. "I did start brainstorming ideas for your wedding, though. Wait until you see what Serge came up with."

Bridget's smile froze, and she began to turn around. Kax held his breath, hoping for her to look at him and see from his face how much he wanted her. Surely she wasn't going to walk away from him without saying goodbye. Not after they'd survived the Kronock together. Not after... everything.

Bridget released a long breath and squared her shoulders. "I hope you told him I don't do blush and bashful."

Mandy threw her head back and laughed. "Don't worry. There's no pink anywhere."

The two women walked arm-in-arm off the flight deck without a backwards glance. Kax felt his shoulders droop even as his brother nudged him.

"I still don't understand the Earth females," Dorn said, his mouth twitching up on one side, "but I do enjoy the one I have."

Kax couldn't help giving his brother a weak smile. Dorn had been the most battle-worn warrior he'd known—rough and tough with lots of hard edges—but he was soft when it came to his mate. Kax hadn't expected the pair to mesh as well as they had, but they seemed to be deliriously happy. He caught sight of a fading bite mark on his brother's neck and raised an eyebrow.

Dorn caught his eyes and reddened slightly. "I have yet to tame her, but we both enjoy the challenge."

Kax shook his head as they headed toward the High Command room. He couldn't be jealous of his brother's happiness. Dorn had given up his command of a battleship on the outskirts of the solar system to take a mate and take Kax's position in the Drexian leadership. While most would consider these to be steps up, he knew Dorn would have preferred the scarred metal of his battleship and the sound of laser fire to the cushy life on the Boat.

"How is the High Command?" Kax asked, as they strode along the pristine corridors, their heavy boots echoing off the curved walls.

Dorn shot him a dark look. "Boring. Remind me to pummel you for leaving our family seat vacant."

"You'll be a valuable addition, brother. They need to hear

from someone who has been engaging the Kronock, especially now."

"They don't want to believe our enemy might have been lulling us into complacency for decades." Dorn let out a breath. "To be honest, I don't want to believe it."

"It isn't your fault or anyone else's. They did a good job of hiding their intentions behind half-hearted attacks. It was impossible to know they were busy building an army of hybrid soldiers and developing sophisticated technology."

"We would have known if we hadn't pulled back on our intelligence," Dorn said. "You told them not to limit the military intelligence units, but they thought it was a waste of resources. They should have listened to you."

Kax shrugged, looking down at the gleaming floors. "We didn't know then what we know now."

Dorn stopped outside the tall, gilded doors leading to the High Command chambers and faced Kax. "What do we know now?"

"It's just a guess, but from what I saw, I suspect the Kronock have been doing medical research for years." Kax said, revealing what he hadn't wanted to in front of the other soldiers. "They've developed highly adept soldier-hybrids, using who-knows-what type of DNA. I suspect they've been harvesting genetic material from the worlds they invade."

"For what purpose?"

Kax raised one shoulder. "I can only suspect they're trying to create superior beings. The Kronock commander who took Bridget is not just Kronock, although I don't know what else he's got in the mix. Something highly intelligent, however."

Dorn frowned. "We need to know when they plan to attack, and how."

"That I can't tell you, but the radioactive material doesn't bode well."

"Agreed," his brother said. "We're sending in a fleet to eliminate the mining colony, so the Kronock won't have that to work with anymore."

Kax felt a sudden pang of sadness for Al, even though he knew it was only a computer program.

"Our next priority must be finding our enemy's research facilities so we can stop them before they develop anything else," Dorn said. "Then we'll send in teams to take them out."

Kax felt a flutter of both excitement and dread. "Send me. I already know the location of a research facility."

"Still able to read my mind, big brother," Dorn said with a shake of his head, as he rested a hand on Kax's arm. "You've had the most recent contact and know what to expect. Of course it's up to you. I told the High Command you'd need a few days to recuperate from your rescue mission."

Kax pushed all thoughts of Bridget from his mind. "I don't need that long. The faster we find out about the invasions and eliminate their advantage, the better."

"There's the Drexian I should be thanking."

Both the booming voice and footsteps made the brothers turn. Karsh, son of Terk, wasn't as tall as Kax or Dorn, but he was broad-shouldered like all Drexian males. He wore his sandy brown hair long, like members of Dorn's Inferno Force did, even though he'd been posted to outposts and battleships that had never seen action. Kax wondered how he'd acquired his sash full of ribbons and medals when he'd never fought in a battle.

"Karsh." Dorn acknowledged him first by clasping the man firmly on the side of the arm. "How long has it been?"

"The last time we saw each other you were headed back to your battleship, and I tried to convince you to accompany me to Zareen."

Kax flinched at the name of the pleasure planet known for

beautiful and willing females, and free-flowing cocktails that eliminated all inhibitions. He narrowed his eyes at Karsh.

"If memory serves me, you had a special attachment to Zareen," Dorn said.

Karsh winked at Dorn. "Her name was Quillan from the empath planet. Anticipates your needs before you know you have them. She spoiled me." He pivoted to face Kax. "But enough about that female. I hear I should be thanking you for bringing my tribute bride home safely."

"Congratulations," Kax said, putting a hand to Karsh's arm. "You are a lucky Drexian."

"Am I?" Karsh squeezed Kax's arm. "I wouldn't know. The human refuses to let me in her suite."

Kax tried not to smile. "Really?"

"Actually, her friend is the one barring my entrance," Karsh said, his eyes resting on Dorn. "Your bride, I believe."

Dorn cleared his throat. "I am sure Mandy is just being protective. Bridget has been through a traumatic experience. She probably needs to rest. Right, brother?"

"Very traumatic," Kax said. "She might need medical treatment, as well."

Karsh frowned. "I was not told she was damaged."

"Nothing permanent." Dorn took him by the arm and spun him toward the High Command doors. "Why don't you join us in the High Command briefing? I'm sure your father would be glad to see you."

Kax followed behind, scrubbing his hand over his face so no one would see the smile he tried fruitlessly to suppress. Knowing Karsh had not seen Bridget made him feel like dancing. Even glancing at the large round table and the solemn faces around it didn't dampen his satisfaction.

CHAPTER TWENTY-THREE

Bridget tossed back the bubbling drink and slammed the empty glass on the bar. "I missed those."

Mandy eyed her as she sipped her own cocktail. "Don't forget what happened the last time we tried these."

"Don't remind me, girl." Bridget remembered all too well. She and Mandy had gotten tipsy and giggly, and Dorn had ended up throwing Mandy over his shoulder and leaving with her. Before Bridget could have another drink, Kax had shown up and escorted her back to her suite almost as forcefully.

Kax. She sighed as she thought of him, letting her mind slip back to their time together on the mining colony. Before they were rescued. Before she was brought back to the Drexian space station and assigned another mate. She licked her lips, the fizzy drink lingering in her mouth.

It had been easier to accept the crazy prospect of being matched up with a huge alien she'd never met back when she'd been convinced love was not for her. She'd known she was in no danger of loving and losing, so it had seemed like a wild adventure. Now, she understood why women hesitated or took a while to wrap their minds around the concept. Bridget couldn't imagine spending her life with some guy she'd never met. Not now. Not after Kax.

Bridget gave her head a small shake, as if trying to expel all thoughts of him from her mind. She took in the holographic environment—golden, sandy beach, cerulean-blue water lapping at the shore, steel-drum music playing instrumental versions of movie theme songs from the 80s. The Boat had a quirkiness she'd grown to like, and the aliens aboard tried hard to make the Earth women happy.

Her gaze fell on the bartender and the small, nubby horns poking out of his wavy blond hair. She knew he wasn't a Drexian, but he was pretty cute. She recognized him from the last time she and Mandy had tossed back cocktails at the tiki bar. That time, they'd made him nervous enough that his tail had twitched up a storm. This time, he seemed more relaxed as he polished a glass.

She caught the bartender's eye and tapped the rim of her glass. "Hit me."

"Well, well." Serge bustled up in a lime-green suit, remarkably similar in color to their drinks, and hopped onto a barstool next to her. "What do we have here? A premature bachelorette party?"

Mandy put a hand on her back. "We're just unwinding a bit. Bridget's been through a lot."

Bridget couldn't see what was going on behind her back, but she could sense Mandy giving the pint-sized wedding planner some pointed looks and perhaps mouthing some things to him.

Serge let out a tortured sigh. "Fine, but I still say there's no time to waste if I'm going to pull together a wedding in three days. Since you're friends with Mandy, and Preston liked her so much, I've sweet-talked him into doing your flowers, but I'm not sure if The King can do another performance so soon. Even with our regenerative medicines, his vocal cords need rest."

Bridget smiled at the bartender as he slid a fresh cocktail toward her. She pulled the round, powder-blue fruit out by the stem and popped it into her mouth. "There was a time when I practically subsisted on the garnishes in my cocktails. Back when I had to stay skinny for the ballet." She chewed on the sweet fruit—a cross in flavor between a cherry and a peach—and the taste exploded on her tongue. "Hold the phone. Did you say three days?"

Serge magically produced a thick, pink binder and slapped it down on top of the bar. "Don't you worry your pretty little head. That's an Earth expression, isn't it?" He waved a hand in the air. "Doesn't matter. I may never have pulled together a wedding in three days, but that doesn't mean it can't be done. We just need to focus and buckle down to work."

Both women stared at him as he opened the binder and flipped to a checklist.

"A binder seems a little old-school, doesn't it?" Bridget asked.

Serge stroked the pages in the binder. "You can't beat a classic."

Mandy glanced at Bridget and reached over, closing the binder and shooting Serge a look Bridget caught.

"Who says it has to be in three days?" Mandy asked.

"The groom has requested it." Serge leaned closer to the women's heads. "He's from one of the most illustrious Drexian families."

Mandy rolled her eyes at Bridget. "Since neither of us had even heard of the Drexian race before a couple of weeks ago, that doesn't blow either of our skirts up. Bridget was kidnapped and just rescued. No way is she ready to walk down the aisle with some complete stranger in three days." Mandy slid her gaze over to hers. "Right?"

Bridget nodded and took a drink. "You can tell Mr. Hot-to-Trot that I'm not."

Serge scratched his head and his purple spiky hair did not move. "My command of the English language is considered exemplary, but I don't understand what that means."

"I already had to kick this guy out when he barged into her suite." Mandy shook her head. "Luckily, Bridget had the bathroom door locked, but he was way too pushy. Even for a Drexian. I mean, I'm all for a big, tough, alpha male, but he needs to give her a little space. This is not a normal tribute bride wedding scenario. And if you see him, tell him Bridget wants her scarf back. He snatched it from the nightstand, and said he'd take it as a token."

Serge cleared his throat. "I'll admit that does seem like a bit much considering."

"You think?" Mandy said.

Bridget motioned to the binder. "Don't you have a section in there about the appropriate amount of time for a wedding after the bride has been abducted and then rescued?"

Serge opened and closed his mouth, his pristinely arched eyebrows disappearing beneath his hair. He stared at the binder, clearly at a loss for words.

Mandy leaned over to Bridget. "Guess not."

Bridget shrugged. "Maybe the binder needs some updating."

Serge sucked in air and ran a hand over the shiny, pink cover. "Bite. Your. Tongue."

Mandy grinned. "You're right. Your command of the English language is excellent."

Serge slid off his barstool and tucked the binder under one arm. "I see I'm getting nowhere with you two. I suppose I'll have to do all the prep work myself and hope we can pull it all together in time." He leveled a finger at first one then the other. "Dress selection tomorrow. No ifs, ands, or buts."

He left in a huff, passing Reina on the way. The tall Vexling walking toward them had a habit of wringing her bony hands in front of her. When she saw Serge, she clasped her hands and began twisting them.

Mandy let out a slow breath. "I'm thinking we should have found a less popular place to drink."

Reina took a seat beside Mandy, casting a final glance at Serge. "I warned him not to rush the planning, but you know how well men listen."

Bridget raised an eyebrow at the woman who'd been assigned first to escort Mandy through the wedding planning process, and had now been assigned to her. "I thought you and Serge were tight."

Reina craned her long neck, looking around at the tropical setting and the smattering of people at the thatched hut poised on a holographic South Pacific beach. She waved at the bartender. "I'll have one of what they're having."

Bridget and Mandy exchanged a look. This was new. Bridget had never seen the usually nervous woman do anything but fret and take it out on her poor hands.

"Serge may be the station's top wedding planner, but he knows nothing about women," Reina said, dropping her voice. "I may not be human, but I know that no female wants to get married right after going through the ordeal you did."

"Thanks, Reina," Bridget said, thinking she may not have given the alien enough credit. "I'm fine, but you're right. I'm not in the mood for a shotgun wedding."

Reina's eyes widened. "Oh, we don't design any weddings with a shotgun theme. Not even for the brides from Texas."

Mandy snorted into her drink.

"I told them you'd need a week at the very least. I was shocked when I heard Dorn's brother was going right back out on a mission, but I'm sure rescuing you wasn't as emotionally taxing for him as it was for you." Reina patted her hand. "After all, you were the one being held by those awful Kronock."

"He's leaving again?" Bridget asked, her voice sounding hollow to her own ears.

Reina eagerly took the cocktail the bartender passed to her, her eyes brightening at the sight of the paper umbrella, blue straw, and floating, blue fruit. "From what I heard he's being sent on a mission to infiltrate Kronock space and try to get information about the Earth invasion."

Bridget swallowed hard. As mad as she'd been at Kax for letting her go so easily, her anger dissolved when she thought of him going on a dangerous mission. She stared into her half empty glass and blinked back tears. Would she ever see him again? Would he even come say goodbye before he left?

"Where did you hear all this, Reina?" Mandy asked.

Reina blushed. "Vexlings have extremely acute hearing, and if I happen to pause near vents, well..."

Mandy elbowed her. "Here I thought you were so prim and proper, and you're covertly listening in on top-secret meetings."

Reina instantly looked panicked. "You aren't going to tell, are you?"

Mandy drew two fingers across her lips and mimed throwing away a key. "Your secret is safe with us, right, Bridget?"

Bridget closed her eyes for a moment, composing herself before turning to the others. "Of course. We would never rat you out, girl."

Reina sank down in the stool, grinning. She lifted her drink with both hands and drained half of the contents with a single gulp from the straw, and then hiccuped. "I feel better already."

"I'll bet you do," Mandy said under her breath.

Bridget pushed her own drink away, her desire for the sweet concoction completely gone. A twisted knot of dread in her stomach had replaced the tingling feeling in her fingers and toes. The thought of Kax in danger made her feel sick. It had been bad enough when he'd been injured on the mining colony, but that was before they'd fallen for each other. Or, at least, before she'd fallen for him. She didn't know what he felt for her, if he'd been fine with her marrying another man and eager to risk his life again against the Kronock.

Even the thought of Kax's hard body and hot nodes made her cheeks flush. As much as she hated to admit it, this was more than a physical connection for her. She knew that now, even if she'd been kidding herself before. She folded her hands on top of the bar and rested her head on them. How could she stay on the space station and marry another Drexian, when her heart already felt like it had left with Kax?

CHAPTER TWENTY-FOUR

The doors swished open, and Kax scanned the inside of the dark officers' club. He didn't know why he was there, except it was the one of the few places on the station where he knew he'd find no tribute brides. Maybe he'd find some solace or some answers. If he was lucky, he'd find his brother.

Even though he'd received his orders from the High Command, Kax didn't seem to be any closer to leaving the station than when he'd left the High Command meeting with his commendation on a successful mission and his instructions for the next one. He'd attempted to pack, but had ended up throwing his bag to the floor. He'd tried to cure himself with a hot shower, but he'd only ended up imagining Bridget's body with him under the pounding water.

Kax ran a hand through his still-wet hair and felt the dampness of his skin against his shirt. That's what he got for stomping out of the bathroom and throwing on clothes without drying off, first. He shook his head, trying to shake the thoughts from the shower out of his mind, as his eyes adjusted to the low lighting.

A shiny, black bar stretched the length of one side of the room with an expanse of floor-to-ceiling windows across the other, giving a stunning view of the distant stars and much closer moons. Square tables clustered tightly together, surrounded by straight back chairs. If music played in the background, Kax couldn't hear it over the murmuring voices. He recognized a few of the officers sitting together—tossing back shots and nursing squat, amber-filled glasses—but he did not see his brother.

Letting out a sigh of exasperation, Kax walked to the bar and ordered a Zimmian whiskey. The bartender, a Vexling in an acid-green vest with a shock of white hair corkscrewing over his head, poured two fingers worth of the vivid, red drink into etched glass and slid it toward him without a word.

Kax slammed back the drink in one gulp, feeling it burn as it slid down his throat, and enjoyed the churning sensation as it hit his stomach. This wasn't Noovian whiskey—smooth and full-bodied. The Zimmians brewed whiskey that burned like acid going down, the pain of the drink replacing any other pain you might have been feeling.

The bartender cocked his head to one side, but Kax shook him off. He had enough experience with Zimmian whiskey to take it slow.

Turning, he leaned back with his elbows against the bar, letting the fire of the whiskey course through his body and dull his senses. If only the alien whiskey had the power to eliminate his feelings, he thought. He took a shuddering breath as his mind went to Bridget—her beautiful wide eyes, her muscular legs, and the full lips that tasted so sweet. But it was the feeling he got when he looked into her eyes that haunted him the most.

He twisted back to the bartender, who hadn't moved from his position, tapping the rim of his empty glass and meeting the Vexling's steady gaze. When the glass held the requisite red whiskey, he raised it in salute and the Vexling nodded. He doubted heartache was anything new for a bartender, especially on a space station designed to facilitate arranged marriages between virtual strangers.

As he lifted the drink to his lips, the doors opened and his eye caught the hulking form of his younger brother.

"There you are," Dorn said, his long strides making short work of the distance between them. "I've been looking everywhere for you. The schematics you requested came through."

He handed a tablet to Kax with a colorful, blinking star chart on the screen.

Kax glanced at it, recognizing the detailed map of Kronock space. He set it down on the bar and leaned his forearms on the reflective black surface, raising the whiskey to his lips.

Dorn watched as he tossed it back in a single gulp, raised an eyebrow, and signaled the bartender with one finger. "Looks like you're trying to drink something away, brother."

Kax gave him a half smile. "Does it matter?"

Dorn shrugged. "Depends on what you're trying to drink away." He lifted his own glass of whiskey, swirling the crimson liquid before taking a sip. "What actually happened at that mining colony?"

Kax closed his eyes, pressing them together and trying to force the memories of Bridget from his mind. Despite his efforts, images of her body splayed on the sheets beneath him filled his mind. "Nothing that makes any difference."

Dorn placed a thick hand on his brother's back. "I'm not so sure."

Kax gave an abrupt shake of his head as he opened his eyes.

"It doesn't matter. Nothing can change the past." He felt his brother's gaze boring into him.

"Maybe not," Dorn said, "but you still have a long future ahead of you, brother. I don't think you want to fill it with years of regret."

Kax whipped his head around so he was facing Dorn. "What do you want me to say? I'm in love with her? I can't stop thinking about someone else's mate?"

Dorn flinched, and Kax saw the anguish in his brother's eyes. He looked away. "Like I said, it doesn't matter. There's nothing to be done about it at this point. I need to forget her and get on with my mission."

Dorn closed his hand around his glass. "From what I hear, you're not the only one having trouble acclimating."

"Why?" Kax asked. "Is she okay?"

Dorn grinned and took a drink. "If you consider getting drunk on pleasure tonic and telling Serge and his wedding planning binder to take a hike, then she's fine."

Kax felt a twinge of pleasure. So Bridget wasn't moving on either. "What about Karsh?"

Dorn turned to glance around the room before lowering his voice. "I don't know much, but I don't think he's even laid eyes on her. I know Mandy has turned him away from Bridget's suite at least once."

Kax's heart did another flip. "Once again, I am glad your mate has such a stubborn streak."

Dorn snorted and clasped a hand on his brother's forearm. "Speaking to you as someone who only recently learned to appreciate what it's like to find your perfect mate, if you have feelings for this woman you need to tell her before it's too late."

Kax knew his brother was right, but his chest tightened

when he thought about telling Bridget everything. "What about...?" he began.

Dorn twitched one shoulder up and stared into his glass. "Who knows? But you're better off telling her and finding out."

Kax gave a small laugh. "When did you become so wise, little brother?"

Dorn winked at him and swallowed the rest of his whiskey. "I must have had a good teacher."

Kax threw his arm around his brother's shoulders, pulling him into a one-armed hug. "I'm glad you came back, even if it was kicking and screaming."

Dorn shot him a look. "I still haven't forgiven you for that you know."

Kax smiled. "Oh, I know. But you haven't thanked me for it yet, either."

Dorn's cheeks colored. "I guess I should thank you. Mandy is the best thing that's ever happened to me."

Kax eyed the fading bite mark on Dorn's neck. "I can see that."

His brother elbowed him then looked down into his glass. "I want the same for you. You deserve it."

Kax did not respond. The words felt stuck in his throat as he thought about Bridget, and the future he may never have.

The bartender held out the skinny bottle of whiskey, the blood-red contents swirling inside. Dorn waved him off. "We've probably had enough."

"Nonsense," A loud voice startled them from behind, and both men felt the slap of a heavy hand on their backs. Karsh had entered the officers club without them noticing and now stood behind them with one hand on each of their shoulders. "I insist on buying another round."

Kax stiffened at the man's touch and let his eyes slide over to his brother's.

Dorn inclined his head at the bartender. "A whiskey for our friend."

"You must join me," Karsh said, lifting his hands from their backs and taking the barstool next to Kax. "You have to help me celebrate."

Dorn raised an eyebrow at Kax while the bartender slid a drink across the bar. "And what exactly are we celebrating?"

Karsh picked up the glass and lifted it high. "My success with my bride." He slugged down the red liquid and slammed the glass on the bar, waving at the bartender for another.

Kax's entire body went rigid, and even Dorn stiffened beside him. "I thought you hadn't been able to see her yet."

Karsh waved a hand dismissively, holding out his glass while the bartender filled it. "She's my mate. She can't deny me."

Kax felt his brother's warning hand on his shoulder.

Karsh swallowed his whiskey in one gulp and turn to them. "Not that she wanted to deny me." He produced a silk scarf and ran the pink fabric through his hands. "Are all the human females so wild?"

The scent of the scarf—Bridget's scent—wafted to his nose and instantly pulled him back to her—the smell of her, the taste of her, the feel of her. Kax's hands shook as he pushed back from the bar and stood.

Karsh grinned at him, clearly enjoying this. "Did you know Earth females like to give tokens of affection to their mates? I guess you wouldn't know much about Earth females though. I'll have to compare notes with your brother."

Before he could say something or do something he would regret, Kax spun on his heel and left the officers' club, pausing to catch his breath once he reached the hallway.

So he *was* too late, he thought. Bridget had accepted her new mate. He'd missed his chance. He dropped his hands to his knees to steady his breath, then pulled himself up to his full height and pounded a fist against the wall until the sting of pain sobered him.

It didn't matter anymore. All he wanted to know was how soon he could leave for his mission.

CHAPTER TWENTY-FIVE

Bridget paced in front of the crackling fireplace in her suite, her bare feet padding across the thick, faux bearskin rug stretched out in front. Snow fell softly on her balcony and moonlight spilled across the frosty slope outside. She glanced at the steaming mug of cocoa on the wooden coffee table. What good was a romantic setting if the only person she wanted to share it with was leaving?

Maybe she should go give Kax a piece of her mind. She stalked toward the door, then stopped. What would she say? He already knew how she felt. She'd spilled her guts when they were stranded on the mining colony. She'd told him everything. Well, not everything, but enough for him to know she wanted him. He knew, and he'd still chosen not to fight for her and instead, go off on a dangerous mission. If she'd learned one thing from surviving foster care and then the cutthroat world of dance, actions spoke louder than words. Kax's actions couldn't have been clearer.

A loud rap startled her and made her pulse race. Maybe he'd wised up and was coming to tell her he'd changed his mind. She threw open the door, preparing to give Kax her most severe look.

It wasn't Kax.

"We brought the wine," Mandy said, as she stepped inside holding up two bottles filled with murky, orange liquid. "Well, not wine exactly, but the closest thing to it."

Reina followed behind Mandy, along with about half a dozen other women she recognized from Mandy's bachelorette party as other tribute brides. All the women carried bottles, wine glasses, or food.

"Mandy thought you needed some company," Reina said, pausing to let the other women walk ahead of her. The Vexling eyed the fireplace and steaming mug. "I hope this isn't a bad time."

Bridget poked her head into the corridor, but it was empty. "Actually, it's perfect timing. I was going out of my mind by myself."

"This isn't your bachelorette party by a long shot," Mandy said, winking at her from across the room where she set out the bottles and wine glasses. "I have lots of other ideas for that, but I thought it was time for some of us tribute brides to have a girls' night."

"Sounds perfect," Bridget said. Anything to take her mind off Kax. She spotted Trista, the other tribute bride from the original game show ruse, where Mandy had been selected as Dorn's mate. Of all the women laughing and smiling, she seemed the most hesitant. Of course, like her and Mandy, Trista had also only been on the space station a little over a week.

"How are you?" Trista asked, walking up.

Bridget felt tears sting the backs of her eyes at the woman's concerned tone. "Fine. I mean, it sucked to be kidnapped for the second time."

"I can imagine." Trista ran a hand through her wavy, blond hair. "I hear those other aliens make these guys really look like a dream."

Bridget laughed and felt her urge to cry fade. "You can say that again."

Mandy appeared with two glasses, and gave Trista a look. "I warned all the girls not to pester you about being kidnapped and rescued and your whole ordeal. They know you were already debriefed and probably don't want to rehash it."

Trista blushed. "Sorry. I didn't mean to..."

Bridget grabbed her hand and squeezed. "I'm fine. I promise." She swallowed hard. It wasn't the kidnapping she wanted to push out of her mind; it was everything that had happened with Kax. She took a sip of the mango-colored drink, and discovered it tasted like Pinot Grigio, but with a slight spicy kick at the end.

Everyone settled on the oversized love seats and chairs curved around the fireplace with Trista taking a place on the fluffy rug and sitting cross-legged. Bridget motioned to Mandy for them to join her, and they plopped down, one on either side. The fire crackled behind them, and Bridget felt the heat against her back.

"It's the original three back together again," Mandy said, nudging Trista.

Trista smiled. "That's right. Hard to imagine it was only a week ago."

Mandy took a drink. "It's crazy how much has happened. Where have you been hiding out, by the way? Aside from my bachelorette party, I don't think I've seen you around the station at all."

Trista looked down at her hands. "It's taken me a while to get used to all this. I was convinced it was all trick."

"That's what I thought until they showed me the view,"

Mandy said. "And when I walked out in the promenade and looked up into space, I realized even LA couldn't recreate this."

Trista sighed. "I'm glad I'm not the only one who thought she was going crazy." She looked from Mandy to Bridget. "Were you two homesick?"

Bridget shook her head. "I didn't have a home to miss, so no."

"At first I thought I missed things about Earth but I realized I really didn't," Mandy said. "My family kind of sucked, so I didn't miss them. What were you homesick for?"

Trista shrugged. "Nothing in particular. Just odd things, like the smell of freshly mown grass, and the sound of crickets chirping at night."

"You lost me there," Mandy said. "I've always lived in LA, but I do miss the sight of all the city lights at night when I'd drive up high on Mulholland."

"And I'd love to hear the hum of South Beach at night again, when all the clubs and restaurants were packed," Bridget said. "It's funny the weird things you miss."

All three women nodded, momentarily lost in their memories.

"No family or friends?" Bridget asked, clearing her throat.

Trista shook her head abruptly. "No one."

Bridget saw something flicker across the woman's face, then disappear. "Then we should toast to new friends."

Mandy raised her nearly empty wine glass. "I'll drink to that."

"What are we drinking to?" Reina asked, as she worked her way toward them holding a bowl and a full glass over her head to keep from spilling.

"You've really embraced cocktails lately," Mandy said, scooting over so Reina could sit next to them.

"Vexlings are normally very dedicated to their work," Reina

said, lowering herself and folding her long legs up underneath her. She passed the bowl filled with some sort of chips to Bridget. "We're what you on Earth would call workaholics, but I figure even I need a bit of a break."

"You do," Bridget said, plucking a dark-purple chip from the bowl. "I can only imagine how hard it is to handle a bunch of human brides."

"And work with Serge," Mandy mumbled into her drink as she also took a chip.

"It's not that I don't enjoy my work," Reina said, sipping her drink, her impossibly long pinky finger extending up as she drank. "But I'd like to do more than just escort humans around."

Mandy patted Reina's leg. "You're much more than an escort."

Reina smiled. "I hope so. I recently submitted a proposal to overhaul the tribute bride selection system, based on the feedback from you girls."

"Us?" Trista looked at the other two women.

"We're hardly girls," Bridget pointed out, munching on the salty chip and wondering if she wanted to know what it was made from.

"You are to me, sweetie," Reina said. "I'm over a hundred of your Earth years."

Mandy almost dropped her glass. "A hundred?" Her eyes went up and down Reina. "You look amazing."

Reina patted her blue hair. "Vexlings live a few hundred years, so I should look good."

Bridget turned slightly, so the warmth of the fire would reach her face, and took another chip. "So what about us 'girls' inspired you?"

"I realized after your reaction to our game show and some

of the elements of the station inspired by your pop culture, perhaps we were in need of some updates."

Mandy held the stem of her glass between her hands as she pressed her palms together in prayer. "Please tell me you're getting rid of the cheesy Dating Game set."

Reina nodded. "That's my suggestion. Its purpose was to ease the transition with something familiar, but I think it's only more confusing."

"Since it's not the 1970s anymore?" Trista said, taking a small handful of chips from the bowl.

"So what will replace it?" Bridget asked, eyeing the addictive purple chips. "How will you match up tribute brides with Drexian warriors?"

"Mandy tells me dating choices are made on earth now by computer programs and by swiping left and right," Reina said.

"You're going to create a Drexian hottie app?" Mandy's eyes shone. "I could definitely help you test that. I know all about which dating apps are the best."

"Not exactly," Reina said, "I did some research and discovered many individuals on those apps are already mated or are deceptive in their images."

"You mean you discovered people are using Tinder and Grindr to cheat, and they're using fake photos to pretend to be hotter than they are?" Mandy said, her tone sarcastic. "You don't say?"

Trista giggled. "I've never gone on those."

"You missed exactly nothing," Bridget said.

"I did suggest we use a computer system to sync up interests like one of your online dating services on earth," Reina continued. "We already use an algorithm and mine data from your governments to locate potential brides. This will just go deeper."

A brunette Bridget recognized from Mandy's bachelorette

party leaned over from the nearest chair. "I wondered how you picked us."

Reina's pale-gray cheeks flushed as more faces swiveled toward her. "I don't know if I should be sharing this."

"Come on," Mandy nudged her. "It's just us girls."

"I didn't write the algorithm," Reina said, "and I don't have anything to do with running it. That's all done in our data and selection center. All I know is it narrows down women who are orphans, only children, or are distant from their families. From there, it eliminates anyone with a close circle of friends or a romantic relationship, although bad romantic relationships don't count."

Mandy laughed. "So if you have a crappy boyfriend, you can get picked just as if you didn't have a boyfriend at all?"

"Yes," Reina said. "We've rescued many women from bad relationships, abusive relationships, or men who were going nowhere."

"I think the Drexians have it all wrong," Bridget said, munching on a chip then taking a sip of the sweet and spicy drink. "If you let the world know you could save women from dead-end relationships and match them up with a big, strapping aliens, I think the females of earth would welcome you with open arms."

Reina shook her head so hard her hair flopped down over her forehead. "Oh, no. We can never tell."

"Just kidding." Bridget patted her arm. "Your secret's safe with us."

One of the blond twins on the couch sat forward. "So tell us about one of the latest tribute brides? You are still bringing up brides, right?"

Reina tapped a finger on her knee. "We paused for safety reasons right after the incursion attempt, but there is one female the data and selection team are considering making an exception for because of her connection to the program already."

"What kind of connection?" Bridget asked. "I thought the whole point was to pick women without connections."

Reina gnawed at her lip. "This woman has a connection to one of you, but you don't actually know her."

Trista dropped her voice. "Like a long lost sibling separated at birth?"

"Like a photographer who's a suspect in Mandy's disappearance," Reina said.

Mandy choked on her drink. "Wait, what? Me? Someone noticed I was gone?" She shook her head. "Why would a photographer have anything to do with it?"

"This woman published a photo of you taken right before you vanished, so the police think she may be involved."

"That's bad luck," Bridget said.

"We feel awful an extraction has had unintended consequences," Reina said. "We work hard to prevent that from happening."

"You can't let her go to jail because they think she kidnapped me, or worse," Mandy said, standing. "You have to bring her here."

Reina looked unsure. "A final decision hasn't been made."

"I'll talk to Dorn," Mandy said, a determined look on her face.

Reina's face dropped another shade. "You can't. If anyone finds out I told you about the inner workings of the tribute bride selection process..." Her words trailed off.

"I'm guessing it wouldn't be good?" Bridget asked.

Reina's sagging shoulders and pinched face were all the answer she needed.

Mandy huffed out a breath. "I can't believe you told me this. I'm not even on Earth anymore, and I'm causing trouble."

She headed for the balcony, wrenching open the sliding door and stepping outside.

"Oh, dear," Reina said, wringing her hands. "I never should have said anything."

"It's okay." Bridget stood and pulled Trista up with her. "We'll talk to her."

Bridget hated that her friend was upset, but talking people off emotional ledges had become one of her specialties. Dancers lived with constant rejection and criticism, and she'd talked more than one friend out of giving up. Besides, dealing with Mandy's problem was much better than having to dwell on hers. She'd do just about anything to keep from feeling like her heart was breaking in two.

CHAPTER TWENTY-SIX

The sound grew louder as Kax rolled over in bed, pulling his pillow around his head to muffle the pounding. It took him a moment to determine the noise wasn't coming from his head, which was a miracle, considering how much he'd drunk the night before. It came from the door to his room, but a room where? He tossed the pillow to the floor, watching as it landed on the smooth, black surface.

Propping himself up on one elbow, he spotted the empty bottle of Noovian whiskey on the nightstand, and the sight of it made his stomach churn. The squat rocks glass next to the bottle still held traces of the green liquid. Kax inhaled deeply and caught a whiff of the potent alien drink, the sharp scent making him taste bile as he slammed a hand over his mouth.

The hammering on the door had not stopped, so he swung his feet to the floor and staggered across the darkened room. Who needed him so badly they were dragging him out of bed in the middle of the night? He waved a palm over the door's side panel and groaned when the door slid back to reveal his brother.

Dorn gaped at him before clamping his dangling mouth shut. "I came to get you for a meeting with the captain."

Kax realized he wore nothing but a snug pair of black underwear and assumed he looked as rough as he felt. "In the middle of the night?"

Dorn crossed his arms and gave him a crooked grin. "It's halfway through a space station morning cycle."

Even though Drexian days were considerably longer, the Boat had been designed to replicate the day and night patterns of Earth. A sunrise and sunset were simulated on the promenade, and lighting throughout the station's corridors and common spaces dimmed in the evening so the humans' body clocks weren't thrown into chaos.

"Morning?" Kax rubbed his temples and waved Dorn inside. "Are you sure?"

Dorn followed him into the room and coughed. "As sure as I am you shouldn't be drinking Noovian whiskey." He picked up the empty bottle and eyed his brother. "I take it this is about Bridget?"

Kax didn't answer as he peeled off his boxer briefs and strode into the bathroom, leaving the door ajar while he touched a panel to activate the shower. Warm water cascaded from the ceiling, and he stepped underneath, the sting of the jets waking him further.

"This isn't like you," Dorn called in. "Drinking alone? Sleeping through meetings?"

Kax leaned his head back and let the water hit his face. He dragged both hands through his hair, trying not to think about the shower at the colony and sharing it with Bridget. He stepped out and shut off the water. Everything he did reminded him of her. He needed to get her out of his mind or he'd go crazy.

Kax toweled off as he walked from the bathroom to the dresser in his bedroom, ignoring his brother leaning against the black desk. After pulling on his uniform pants and jacket, he turned and managed a smile.

"A lapse that won't happen again," he said.

Dorn didn't look so convinced. "If it's too soon for you to go back out there, we can find someone else. No one will fault you for wanting a break after your rescue mission."

Kax shook his head and passed Dorn on the way to the door. "And stay around here watching her with *him*?" His lip curled as he thought of Karsh. "Should I attend their wedding, as well?"

Dorn followed into the corridor, the door to Kax's quarters sliding closed behind them. "When you put it that way, maybe a mission is just what you need. I know nothing improves my mood like battling the enemy."

They walked without speaking; the echo of their heavy boots the only sound in the pristine hallways. Both nodded when they passed a Vexling bustling along next to a tribute bride, and pounded a fist to their chests when they passed fellow Drexian warriors in uniform. They rode the inclinator in silence, or as close to silence as they could get with faint instrumental music wafting overhead.

"I forgot to ask earlier," Kax said when they reached the wide doors leading to the bridge. "Do I look presentable?"

Dorn waved a palm next to the door. "A question you probably should have asked me before now." He gave a backward grin as he walked through the sliding doors and onto the bridge.

Kax cursed his brother under his breath and followed, throwing back his chest and hoping confidence would make up for his less-than-polished appearance. The dark interior of the station's bridge was a welcome change from the bright lights of the hallways, and he watched officers standing and moving around ebony-colored consoles.

Captain Varden crossed toward them, his own uniform boasting sharp creases, and the streaks of silver at his temples adding to his air of authority. "Commanders, thank you for coming."

Kax and Dorn followed him over to a large, computerized star chart. Lights blinked and blue-arced paths indicated orbits and trajectories on the clear panel. Kax squinted as he tried to make sense of the dots and lights.

"You said it was urgent," Dorn said.

The captain nodded. "Since the incursion and the abduction, we've been on high alert. As you know, it's been decades since any sort of contact with the Kronock this close to Earth. To be honest, our defenses weren't ready, and it's taken some work to get our systems up to a level I'm satisfied with." He pointed to Earth on the chart and the curved lines extending from it to the red dot indicating the Boat. "We've resumed our tribute bride transports, but added significant security measures. Our fighter pilots are flying a consistent orbit around the station, and we have long-range ships patrolling between us and the outskirts."

Kax cleared his throat. "That all seems good."

Captain Varden clasped his hands behind his back. "For now. I'm concerned about what happens when the enemy comes at us with a full attack."

"If you're telling me you don't think the attack on the station was a full attack," Dorn said, "then I agree."

"We've gotten reports from Inferno Force that the Kronock are moving ships to the outskirts," the captain continued. "Battleships. Lots of them."

Kax's stomach tightened. He'd seen the enemy's new battleships, and they were impressive. It had only been with luck and some guerrilla tactics that they'd been able to destroy them during the last battle. He didn't like thinking of a fleet of battleships coming for them.

"Do you want Inferno Force to engage?" Dorn asked. Inferno Force was the fleet he'd led before being summoned to the Boat to take a mate. They were considered the roughest and toughest of the Drexian warriors, and also the most victorious ones.

"Not and be blown out of the sky," Kax said. "You saw the new battleships, brother. If they have an entire fleet of them, Inferno Force, as good as they are, will be outgunned."

Dorn scowled, clearly not pleased to think anything could outmatch his warriors, but he didn't argue.

"We still have stealth technology the Kronock don't seem to posses, although I suspect they are trying very hard to acquire it," Captain Varden said.

"Why do you say that?" Kax asked.

"We just got word they captured a Drexian science vessel. Luckily, the science team had nothing to do with stealth technology or military research of any kind, so the information remains safe."

"And the Drexians on the science vessel?" Kax asked, bracing himself for the answer.

"Dead," the captain said. "The Kronock ripped the ship apart and then slaughtered the entire crew when they realized it wasn't what they'd been searching for. We know this because one security officer managed to hide and get off a transmission before he was found."

Dorn balled his hands by his sides and emitted a low growl.

Kax tried to keep his rage in check. "So we still have the

advantage of stealth cloaking, but we don't have the army to match the one they've been building?"

"And as soon as our stealth ships fire, the advantage is eliminated," Dorn reminded him.

"The Kronock commander who was after..." Kax paused, "the tribute bride, said they intended to attack Earth. We know this for a fact. Since he seemed to want human DNA to somehow aid with their invasion, I'd hoped his failure to harvest it would have slowed down the timeline."

Dorn rocked back on his heels. "Do we know he didn't get it?"

Kax swung his head around. "What?"

"Bridget said she *thought* they didn't get anything from her, but she admitted she was sedated twice," Dorn said. "And you reported you saved her from a research building. Who's to say they hadn't already harvested her human DNA?"

"Then why did they come after us?" Kax said, but he knew the answer to his own question, even if he didn't want to admit it to the others. It was because Krav had developed an obsession with Bridget, beyond using her for their military plan. He'd seen it in the creature's face and heard it in his voice. He wanted her in the same way Kax wanted her.

Dorn shrugged. "Because they're animals."

Kax forced himself not to think Bridget could still be in danger. "So what do we do? We can't let the Boat fall into Kronock hands, and we can't let Earth be invaded."

"Reinforcements from the home world are on their way," Captain Varden said, "and I've taken the liberty of putting Inferno Force on the highest alert. They're our first line of defense. We don't know how or when the enemy will attack, but my gut tells me it's coming sooner than we thought."

"We need to know their plan," Kax said, more to himself than to the two men. The only way to keep Bridget truly safe was to stop the Kronock invasion and cut their technological research off at the knees. He straightened his shoulders. "I need to go now."

Dorn shook his head. "The intelligence team isn't fully assembled, and we haven't determined targets."

"We don't have time to wait," Kax said. "Not with an invasion imminent. You know I'm right, brother."

Dorn raked a hand through his hair and it flopped back in his face. "You can't mean to go solo?"

Kax nodded. "It's the best way for me to get into enemy space undetected. I did it once. I'll do it again."

Captain Varden frowned. "We don't know where a Kronock centralized command might be, if they even have one. It could take more time than we have to determine the most high priority targets."

Kax took a step back, thinking of the black armored Kronock on the colony as he'd stalked onto his ship and fired off orders. "I know exactly where to hit them."

CHAPTER
TWENTY-SEVEN

Bridget gasped when she and Trista joined Mandy on the balcony and the cold air hit them. "Girl, it's freezing out here."

"You're the one who picked a ski chalet suite," Mandy said, not turning around.

"Technically I didn't pick it. Reina picked it for me," Bridget said, stepping over to the wooden railing and rubbing her arms. "But I probably would have picked it anyway. I may have lived in Miami, but I've always loved the snow." She jerked a thumb behind her. "The key is watching it from the inside."

"If you came out here to make me feel better, it won't work," Mandy said. "Everything up here was going so great, and then I get reminded of my old life and told I'm the reason someone else's life may be ruined. What am I supposed to do with that?"

Bridget rubbed a hand over Mandy's back. "It's not your fault. None of us planned to be taken by aliens, right? Who knows what's really going on back on Earth without us? For all I know, there could be search parties looking for me." She seriously doubted it, since everyone probably suspected she'd skipped town as soon as she'd been cut from the ballet.

Trista shivered and moved her hands briskly up and down her arms. "It doesn't matter. They'll never find you."

"Exactly," Bridget said. "We're out of reach now, which also means we can't go around feeling guilty about what we may have left behind."

Mandy grumbled and shook her head. "You'd think the Drexians have been doing this long enough to know how not to set off a chain of horrible events."

"We don't know it's horrible," Trista said. "I'm sure everything will turn out for the best."

Mandy eyed the woman. "Are you always this positive?"

Trista looked down. "Not always."

"I'm sorry." Mandy slipped her arm through Trista's. "I like it. It's good for me to remember not everyone is cynical like they are in LA."

"Or as mercenary as they are in the dance world," Bridget said.

Trista shuffled her feet in an obvious attempt to keep warm. "At least one part of your life is great. You and Dorn seem happy."

"True." Mandy cast her a sideways glance. "I guess I'm being a bit of a drama queen, aren't I?"

Bridget held up two fingers to indicate a small amount.

Mandy's shoulder drooped. "I'm sorry. Old habits die hard, I guess. I have nothing to complain about, when neither of you have even met your guys, or know if you're going to like them."

"I'm terrified mine will think I'm not glamorous enough," Trista said, her words choked.

"What?" Mandy spun on her. "What are you talking about? Men love blondes."

Trista gave a shake of her head. "I feel way out of my league up here. Before this, I'd never even flown on a plane."

"Your first flight was an alien abduction?" Mandy gave a low whistle. "That's harsh."

Bridget put her arm around the woman. "None of that matters anymore. None of us are sophisticated compared to the aliens up here. I'm sure your Drexian will be thrilled with you."

"What about you?" Trista asked, clearly trying to change the subject. "Do you think you'll fall for your guy like Mandy fell for hers?"

Bridget smiled, the words stuck in her throat. How could she tell them she'd already fallen for a Drexian but he hadn't fallen for her?

"Bridget doesn't believe in true love or soul mates," Mandy nudged her. "Right?"

Bridget tried to laugh it off, but her laugh became a sob.

"What's wrong?" Mandy wrapped her arms around her. "I was only joking."

Bridget waved her off. "I'm being silly. I don't know why I'm crying. You're right. I never believed in love or soul mates or any of that."

Mandy held her at arm's length and studied her. "But now you do?"

Bridget shrugged. "I don't know. I feel like I'm all mixed up. My stomach is in knots. I feel like throwing up. I can't focus on anything."

"You're in love!" Mandy threw her arms around Bridget. "This is so exciting!"

"What? No," Bridget gave a brusque shake of her head. "I can't be in love. It feels like torture."

Trista nodded. "Sounds like love to me." She cocked her

head to one side. "But I thought you hadn't met the Drexian warrior they matched you with yet."

Mandy's mouth opened in a perfect *O* as her eyes widened. "It's not Karsh. It can't be. Trista's right. You haven't even laid eyes on him." Her voice dropped to a whisper. "You're in love with Kax, aren't you?"

Bridget's cheeks burned and tears threatened the backs of her eyes. "Neither of us meant for anything to happen."

Mandy clapped her hands. "This is so exciting. If you marry Dorn's brother, we'll officially be sisters."

"I wouldn't count on that," Bridget said. "You know how the Drexians are about their matches."

Mandy frowned. "Don't be ridiculous. If you and Kax are in love, they can't make you marry someone else. It's not like Kax is some sort of untouchable. He's Dorn's brother, and he was a member of their High Command. I'm sure a big shot like him can pull a few strings."

Bridget gnawed on her bottom lip, but didn't reply.

"Does he know how you feel?" Trista asked, her eyes not leaving Bridget's face.

"I might not have told him I'm in love with him, but he knows I want him."

"Do you know if he feels the same way about you?" Trista continued.

Bridget looked up at the artificial night sky to keep the tears from spilling down her cheeks. "I don't know. I thought he did, but he didn't fight for me when he found out about Karsh. Maybe it was just sex for him."

Mandy's face fell. "You told him you want him and he's still leaving? I can't believe that." She shook her head. "It doesn't make sense. Why would any sensible man want to leave you? Are you sure he heard you?"

Bridget couldn't help smiling through her tears at her friend's loyalty. "He knows I want him. The truth is, he doesn't want me as much as I want him, and I need to learn to deal with it and move on, even if it feels like I'm being ripped in two."

"Oh, Bridge." Mandy wiped at her own tears. "I'm so sorry. Do you want me to have Dorn talk to him? Or knock some sense into him?"

"No," Bridget laughed. "But I appreciate the offer. I don't want anyone who has to be talked into being with me." She squared her shoulders. "I just need to go back to my old mindset. I didn't believe in love before. Marrying someone I don't love will be much easier if I remember that."

She knew that was easier said than done. Since she'd experienced the rush of falling in love, she didn't know if it was possible to go back. Or if she even wanted to.

CHAPTER TWENTY-EIGHT

Kax focused his eyes on the familiar planet as his ship came out of the jump. When he'd escaped with Bridget a few days earlier, he never would have imagined he'd be returning to Choor Dar so soon. If he was being honest with himself, he wasn't sure if he was ready for this mission. He'd barely recovered from the last one.

He put a hand to his chest where he'd been wounded, and his mind went to Bridget. He dropped his hand and tried to push those thoughts away. No use thinking about a woman who was mated to another. He needed to have his head in the game, if he was going to succeed on his mission. And he *had* to succeed, unless he wanted Earth and the Boat to be invaded and harvested by the Kronock.

As he'd done last time, he entered the hazy brown atmosphere quickly, dropping through the radiation before he could be detected. He held his breath, waiting for incoming fire, but none came. His stealth mode had held. Instead of landing where he had before, he chose a spot on the other side of his target building. It would be a longer walk, but a high rock overhang would hide him from view if he lost stealth coverage. He touched down and disengaged the engines, casting a glance at the unforgiving terrain out the front before donning his environmental suit.

Once he'd pulled on the snug-fitting outfit, Kax flipped up the hood, tapping his wrist control and starting the oxygen flow while he also double-checked his directional guidance system. He would be approaching the building from the north this time, and if he remembered correctly from his last visit, the room outfitted with computers—the one he counted on to contain their records—was located on the north side.

Kax left the shuttle, closing the ramp behind him, and allowing himself a moment to adapt to the rough wind and swirling dirt. He glanced at his wrist again and began running, keeping low as he rounded an outcropping of boulders, grateful his suit's color adapted to the surroundings and made him harder to detect. Instead of cutting through a door's bolt, this time he hoped to find a more inconspicuous way to gain entrance. Since he wasn't doing a snatch-and-grab, he did not want to announce his presence so soon.

As he closed in on the building, he noticed a stream of soldiers loading crates onto shuttles at the opposite end. Looked like someone was leaving in a hurry, he thought. Well, not before he got what he needed.

Kax spotted a blacked-out window midway up one wall. Taking a running leap, he clasped the bottom ledge and pulled himself up until he lay flat on the ledge, using his hands and feet to keep him wedged onto the narrow space. He pressed one hand against the glass and jerked it back, snapping the locking mechanism and sliding it back enough for him to drop inside.

The room was dark, and Kax slid the window closed, hearing no alarms. He flipped back his hood and face mask, breathing in the antiseptic air. If he hadn't already known this was a research facility, the scent would have been a dead give-away. As before, he was struck by the lack of security measures. Either the Kronock were extremely confident in their ability to mask their presence, they believed in their ability to defeat any attackers, or they were setting a trap. He swallowed hard and hoped it was not the latter.

After getting his bearings and listening at the door, he crept out of the room and down the hall. The lights were dim and the place seemed deserted. Maybe he'd been wrong, and this was not the place the Kronock commander had ordered his men to return to. It had been loud as all the ships blasted off from the abandoned mining colony, after all. He continued to the room he'd remembered as having computers, feeling a jolt of satisfaction when he saw a wall of whirring machines and a standing console.

"Please be here," he whispered as he activated the console and began typing on the keyboard. He'd learned enough of the Kronock language to recognize the room was indeed where they housed records from their experiments. As he scanned the documents, his stomach churned. Hundreds of species were listed, and Kax realized how many planets their enemy had invaded and how much DNA they'd assimilated. He saw diagrams of grafts they'd made to their people and to splices they'd made to their own genome. Without being an expert in either the Kronock language or genetics, he didn't know the full implication, but he suspected it wasn't great.

His eyes caught on the Kronock word for Drexian, and his mouth went dry as he realized the Kronock had harvested DNA from his people. Then he saw the word for Earth, and his mouth went dry. Had they harvested DNA from Bridget without her knowing? He wanted to scan further, but knew he needed to hurry.

Kax took a small metal disc from the pocket of his suit and pressed it to the console. If it worked properly, it should download all the files so he could get them back and have them officially translated. The disc flashed green, and Kax let out a breath. It was working. After a few minutes, the disc glowed yellow and then red. Kax removed it from the console and zipped it into his pocket.

A sound from the doorway made him look up. A Kronock had entered the room, one of the less mechanized versions with only small flashing lights at the base of his scaly neck. Kax pulled a blaster off his belt and shot before the enemy could raise the alarm. Luckily, the creature had not been a soldier wearing armor, so the shot to the chest leveled him. As he eyed the Kronock bleeding out on the floor, Kax suspected he was a scientist or paper pusher of some kind, since he'd had no weapon, and seemed genuinely shocked to see an intruder.

Kax knew he should get out as quickly as possible, but he needed to do one more thing. He managed to pull up a schematic of the building on the console, tapping his finger on the room in the corner. It wasn't far, although he didn't see an easy escape from that side of the building. He steeled himself. He had to do this to keep Bridget safe.

Running out of the room and down the hall, Kax kept his blaster held high, hoping he'd run into more scientists and none of the enhanced fighters he'd met during the incursion. He found the lab, although his heart sank when he saw it had already been partially packed up. He eyed a clear box filled with test tubes. There was no time to locate Bridget's sample, if there was one and if it was even there. He took a small device from his pack and attached it to the underside of one of the metal tables. He activated it and rushed out.

Running faster now, he ducked into stairwell as the doors

of an inclinator opened, hurrying down the darkened stairs until he reached the level below. So far, so good.

Kax emerged onto the floor, sweeping his blaster one way and then the next but seeing no movement. A niggling voice in the back of his head told him if the place was really as deserted as it felt, he wouldn't find who he was after. Would the General stay around as his facility was dismantled?

Glancing at his wrist, he noted how much time he had remaining and determined which way to go, racing down the hall on the balls of his feet. The door on the end stood open, and voices came from within. It was the harsh guttural sounds of Kronock, and one voice he recognized.

Kax pulled the photon grenade off his belt, and his pulse quickened. He'd only have a few seconds after throwing it to get clear of the blast zone. Even at his fastest run, he might not make it without injury. He clenched his fist around the black orb. If it guaranteed Bridget's safety, it would be worth it.

He stepped out into the open doorway, taking in the scene inside the room in a second. Krav stood with his hands resting on a wide console, as he spoke to another Kronock, this one with his back to Kax. The commander stopped when he saw Kax, his lip curling into a sneer.

Kax pressed the detonation sequence on the three buttons on the grenade. "Catch." He tossed it inside the room as the other Kronock turned toward him. Kax faltered as he spun to leave. The other creature wasn't Kronock. At least, not completely. Scars crossed his humanoid face, but the eyes were a shocking shade of blue, and the gray scales on his bare arms looked patchy.

Run, he told himself, as he pushed the confusing thoughts from his mind and sprinted down the hall. The precious seconds he'd lost because of his hesitation meant he felt the heat of the blast as the grenade blew. Kax's body was propelled forward, and he slammed into a wall, debris raining down over him as he shielded his head with his arms. Bellowing and screaming echoed through the air as the acrid smell of burning flesh hit his nose. Staggering to his feet, Kax stumbled away.

He had to get to his ship. He'd just killed one of the Kronock leaders, and they would be coming after him. And someone else. He'd also killed someone else. He ran up the stairs and located the window he'd used to enter the building. He flipped up his protective hood and face mask then slid back the glass and dropped down to the ground, swallowing the tang of blood as he landed hard. Another blast from inside the building rocked him, and he struggled to stand.

His feet pounded on the dry dirt as he ran to his ship and tried to convince himself he hadn't seen what he thought he had. It must have been his mind playing tricks on him. No way the bumps he'd seen through the back of the thin, white shirt of the other creature in the room had been nodes.

Kax opened the ramp of his ship and didn't slow as he ran aboard. He sank into the pilot's chair, his hands shaking. *Grek. Did I just murder a Drexian-Kronock hybrid?*

CHAPTER TWENTY-NINE

Bridget looked down at the pile of satin and tulle, and groaned inwardly. She stood in the well-lit dressing room, with a standing mirror on one side and a cream-colored, tufted chair next to it. Muzak played overhead, and Bridget could have sworn it was the instrumental version of the *The Beauty and The Beast* soundtrack.

How had she let them talk her into wedding planning, when she hadn't even laid eyes on her intended mate? She knew Kax had left the ship on a mission he might not return from, and even if he did return, he'd made it clear he didn't want her. Bridget had learned early on in life to be pragmatic. She couldn't think of a good reason not to accept her new Drexian match and get on with it. So why did she hate even thinking about a wedding that didn't include Kax standing at the other end of the aisle? And since when had she started having fantasies about her wedding?

"This one doesn't look too bad," Mandy said, holding up a lace sheath dress with a mermaid skirt.

Bridget barely glanced at it. "Mm-hm. Pretty."

"Um, Bridge," Mandy dropped the dress back into the pile. "Are you sure you want to be doing this?"

Bridget gave her a weak smile. "What's the alternative?"

Mandy sighed, but Serge's sharp rap on the door prevented her from answering.

"How are we doing in there?" he called, his voice a high-pitched chirp.

"Fine," Mandy said, rolling her eyes conspiratorially at Bridget. "Don't worry. I was a mess when I picked out a dress. Actually, most of my wedding planning was a mess. I barely knew Dorn, and I wasn't happy about any of it."

"Barely is better than not at all," Bridget said. "Anyway, you two seem to have gotten to know each other pretty fast."

Mandy blushed. "He's pretty amazing. I never thought I'd meet someone I'd feel this way about."

Bridget felt a rush of warmth for her. The two women hadn't known each other long, but being snatched from Earth by a race of alien warriors had given them something major in common.

Bridget picked up one of the dresses and held it high. "I think I saw this dress on an old *Dynasty* rerun."

Mandy giggled, putting a hand over her mouth to muffle the sound. "Yeah, they're a little dated in their fashion up here. The good news is Randi and Monti will do just about anything you ask. The dress I wore on my wedding day was a custom design."

Bridget looked hard at the pile of gowns Randi and Monti—the Boat's colorful gown designers—had selected for her. She couldn't imagine wearing any of these dresses. Actually, the problem was, she couldn't imagine being the bride if Kax wasn't the groom. Not that he'd ever said he wanted to marry her. Actually, he'd been pretty clear from the beginning that they had no future together. She could never say the guy wasn't brutally honest. Unfortunately, he was also brutally gorgeous and had stolen her heart.

Mandy waved her hands in front of her face. "Earth to Bridget."

"Sorry, girl," Bridget said. "I'll focus. I promise." She wrinkled her nose as she fingered a shiny taffeta skirt. "Do they have anything that won't blind the guests?"

Mandy stuck her head out of the dressing room. "Can we have some non-satin options?"

Murmuring was followed by the shuffling of feet, and moments later the door was flung open. Serge bustled in, holding two dresses on hangers. He wore a three-piece, banana-yellow suit with shiny, platform shoes to match.

"Neither of these are satin," he said.

Mandy gaped at him. She reached out and touched one of the dresses. "What is this? Spandex?"

Serge frowned at her, putting both hands on his slim hips. "You said no satin. These aren't satin."

Bridget smiled at him and took the dresses, placing them over the tufted chair. "I'll give them a try. Thanks, Serge."

"Just trying to help, darling." Serge gave her a smile, shot Mandy a look, and hurried out of the room with his purple hair bobbing.

"Is this a romper?" Mandy asked, holding out one of the non-satin options like it was nuclear waste. "I'm going to have to have a talk with Randi and Monti."

Bridget stepped out of her blue sundress, stripping down to her panties and strapless bra. "It's fine. I need to try on something. We've been here for an hour already. Maybe it will look better on."

"It can't look worse," Mandy muttered.

Bridget slipped on the simplest looking gown, an ivory sheath with spaghetti straps and a lace overlay.

Mandy tapped a finger on her chin, flipping her long, chestnut-brown hair off her shoulder. “It’s not hideous, but it seems a bit understated for you. Since you were a ballerina, I always imagined you in something floaty. You know, with tulle and a long train.”

Bridget ran a hand over the lace of the dress and it scratched her fingers. “This isn’t exactly what I imagined my wedding gown looking like.”

“Yoo-hoo!” Serge called. “Any progress?”

“We’re dying out here,” another voice said, either Randi or Monti, but Bridget didn’t know which.

“I’m going to let them see.” Bridget pushed the dressing room door open, and walked out into the bridal salon.

The two dress designers rushed up to her and began fidgeting with the dress, pulling on it and tugging. Both wore all-black suits with high collars. One had gold hair and matching eyeliner, while the other alien had metallic-silver hair pulled in a low ponytail. Bridget had already forgotten who was Monti and who was Randi, but she suspected those weren’t their real alien names.

Serge put both hands to his cheeks and inhaled sharply. “You’re a vision.”

Bridget allowed herself to be led to the circular platform, surrounded by floor to ceiling mirrors. Stepping up, she saw herself from all angles. The platform levitated a few inches off the ground and began rotating slowly. Ignoring the dress not fitting properly, she didn’t look like what she imagined happy brides to look like. As she met her own eyes in the mirror, she blinked away tears.

Reina, who’d been quiet all morning, came up and handed her a tissue.

“Don’t you start crying,” Serge said. “You know if you start, I’ll start.”

How could Bridget tell them she wasn't crying tears of joy over getting married? She was crying because she'd lost the only guy she'd truly cared about. She dabbed at her eyes and took a steady breath.

"Are you saying yes to the dress?" Randi or Monti asked, as both men bounced up and down on their toes.

Bridget took a final look at the dress and shook her head. "No, I'm definitely not saying yes to this dress."

She couldn't bear watching their eager faces fall as she hopped off the platform before it stopped moving and walked back into the dressing room, passing Mandy on the way. Before the door had closed behind her, she whipped the dress over her head and tossed it into the pile. "I can't do this."

Mandy looked at her. "The dress shopping or the wedding?"

"Both," Bridget said. "I can't marry Karsh."

Mandy bit the edge of her lower lip. "I know it's been rough with your first fiancé killed in battle and then with you being abducted, but don't you think you should at least meet the guy? You know no one wanted you and Kax to happen more than me, but he left. He made his choice."

"I know that rationally, but it doesn't matter to my heart," Bridget said. "This Karsh could be the greatest guy in the world, and he wouldn't stand a chance. I've already fallen for someone, and I can't do anything about it. This is exactly why I always said love is stupid."

Mandy laughed. "I won't argue with you there. Love makes you do dumb things."

The dressing room door swung open, and both women stared as a Drexian warrior strode in, holding an oversized bundle of crimson flowers.

"What the hell?" Mandy said.

Bridget fumbled to pick up her sundress from the floor and

held it in front of her as the alien looked her up and down, clearly enjoying her nearly naked state. The sound of Serge spluttering in shock came from outside the dressing room, and eventually she saw his purple hair popping up behind the uniformed warrior.

"Allow me to introduce your fiancé," Serge said, his voice even higher and tighter than usual.

Karsh gave a small bow without taking his eyes off her, and he licked his lips. "I've waited a long time to see this."

Mandy stepped in front of Bridget and put both hands on the man's wide chest, leaning into him and attempting to push him out. "Well, you're going to have to wait a little longer. You can't just barge in when someone is dressing."

Karsh flicked his eyes down to her. "I can when it's my mate."

Any illusions Bridget had held about her new fiancé were ruined. She met his eyes and narrowed her own. "I am not your mate."

His grin faltered. "Not yet, but soon."

Bridget pulled the sundress over her head and smoothed it down along her hips. She pushed past him, out of the dressing room, and caught a glimpse of Randi's and Monti's open-mouthed surprise as she barreled past them. She didn't stop until she stood outside on the idyllic, cobbled sidewalk in the perfectly designed shopping square.

She heard the clip-clop of Serge's platform shoes behind her as he called her name. "Where are you going? You haven't picked out a dress, and the wedding is in two days."

Bridget spun around and saw that Karsh had followed her out of the salon, along with Serge, Mandy, Randi, and Monti. She looked at the expressions, ranging from shocked to horrified to smug. She balled her hands into fists. "I'm going back to my suite."

Karsh stepped forward. "I'll join you."

Bridget's blood began to boil as she saw the confident, almost arrogant, expression in his eyes. No way she was being mated to this guy. Not even if it meant living in the worst part of the space station, with all the other reject tribute brides.

"I don't think so." She said, watching Mandy's lips curl up into a smile and Serge's open into a perfect circle of surprise.

"What do you mean?" Karsh asked. "You are my mate." He took another step forward. This time, *his* fists were clenched and his expression stormy.

"Not if I reject the match," she said.

"You can't do that," he said. "You'll be an outcast."

Bridget shrugged. "Won't be the first time."

Karsh took several long strides to reach her until he towered above her, his face red with fury. "You will be mine."

"I don't think so, buddy."

"Now, now," said Serge, his voice trembling. "Let's all calm down and take a deep breath. I'm sure we can talk this out."

"I'm perfectly calm," Bridget said. "And there's nothing to talk out. I can't marry him."

Karsh grabbed her arm tightly and she yelped from the pain of it. "You are mine, human, and you're coming with me."

Bridget tried to jerk her arm away from him, but his grip was too firm.

"She said no." Mandy flew at him from behind with her arms outstretched.

The impact of her jostled him, but he only released his grip slightly. When Reina knocked into him, however, it was another matter.

Bridget hadn't even seen the willowy woman leap into action before she hit Karsh from the side and he went stumbling across the cobbled square and straight into the burbling stone fountain.

The Drexian looked stunned, as he sat waist-deep in water, with the stone cherub tinkling water on his head. Bridget and Mandy both stared at Reina with new appreciation.

She brushed her palms together. "Vexlings are known for unusual strength, we just choose not to exploit it."

Bridget's heart rate began to steady as she looped her arm through the blue-haired alien's. "Girl, if I was that strong, I'd be exploiting the hell out of it."

Serge looked from Reina to Karsh, his eyes rolling back into his head before he fainted dead away. Monti and Randi both darted forward to catch him, each holding one floppy banana-yellow arm.

Mandy shook her head. "I guess it finally sunk in that he doesn't have a wedding to plan."

CHAPTER THIRTY

"Thank the gods," Dorn said, coming aboard the shuttlecraft, breathing as if he'd run a race. "I heard you were coming in on fumes."

Kax managed to smile for his brother. "I took some fire as I escaped from Kronock space. They had half a fleet waiting for me as I lifted off the planet. I barely jumped away in time."

"I take it the mission wasn't as covert as you'd hoped?"

"I decided to take out a high-value target," Kax said. "Once I dropped a photon grenade in his lap, my low profile was blown."

Dorn glared at his brother, then his face broke into a smile and he pulled him into a hug. "You lucky bastard."

Kax gave a small laugh. "Lucky? I almost got blown to bits."

Dorn pushed him away. "Stop taunting me. You know how much I miss the fighting." He looked around the cramped ship. "I miss being in command. I miss having a ship. I miss the danger."

"If you want to run in front of me, I'm happy to shoot at you."

Dorn rolled his eyes and jabbed an elbow in his brother's side. "You want to tell me what's going on with you?" He motioned to his brother's scorched hair and burned suit. "This isn't your typical MO."

Kax turned away. "It's nothing that has to do with the mission."

"Then why do you look like you tried to get yourself killed and are miserable you didn't succeed?" Dorn asked.

Kax clenched his teeth, trying not to snap. "I'm fine. Now do you want to join me when I brief the High Command?"

Dorn pressed his lips together and nodded. "Nothing I'd like better, aside from a full-scale battle, of course." A device on his belt began beeping, and he groaned as he pulled it off and peered down at the small screen.

Kax couldn't help grinning. "Trouble in paradise?"

Dorn looked down at the letters scrolling across the screen and shook his head. "It's times like these I remember why I hate being on the Boat."

Kax picked up the tablet with the downloaded battle plans. His brother's marital issues were none of his business, even though it amused him.

Dorn made a series of unintelligible grunts as he typed out a message in return. "I hope this doesn't have too much blow-back. The last thing I want to deal with is an angry member of the High Command."

"What does your wife have to do with the High Command?"

"Not her," Dorn said. "It's Bridget. She's rejected Karsh and refused to go through with the wedding."

Kax's heart contracted, but he worked to steady his voice. "Can she do that after they've...?"

Dorn flicked his gaze to him. "I think we can assume Karsh lied about the progression of their relationship. No tribute bride can be forced into something she doesn't want. You know that as well as I do, brother. Of course, the alternative isn't great for her, but Mandy says she's determined."

"I'll bet Karsh isn't happy," Kax said, smiling in spite of himself.

Dorn tilted his head at his brother. "That's probably an understatement, knowing Karsh." Dorn read his next incoming message.

"I better get over there. Mandy says it's a disaster. Bridget is packing to move to the other side of the station, Serge is hysterical, and my mate is trying to lodge a formal protest to keep Bridget in the fantasy suites." Dorn put a hand to his forehead and rubbed it. "Sometimes I wish my mate wasn't so much of a wildcat."

"I doubt that," Kax said, knowing how much his brother liked a challenge.

Dorn grinned at him. "Maybe you're right, but I really wish she and Reina hadn't pushed Karsh into a fountain."

This got better by the minute, Kax thought. He loved the idea of the arrogant Karsh being humiliated. "Did she say why?"

"She says they were defending Bridget when Karsh got rough with her."

Kax's blood heated, as he imagined the man putting his hands on Bridget. He handed the data disc to Dorn and balled his hands into fists. "This should be the information we need. I need to go. There's something I have to take care of."

Dorn looked his brother up and down. "Do you need a wing man? Or a second?"

"No." Kax flexed his fists. "I've got this."

CHAPTER
THIRTY-ONE

"I can't believe I did that," Reina said, fluttering her hands in front of her face as she paced small circles around Bridget's fantasy suite.

Serge peeked out from under the arm he'd draped across his face, lifting his head from the chaise lounge he lay stretched across. "I can't believe you did that, either." He slumped back down. "He's the son of one of the most powerful Drexians."

"Well, I'm thrilled you did it," Bridget said, as she pulled clothes from the dresser and walked them over to the suitcase flopped open on the king-size bed.

Reina gave her a tentative smile. "It did feel pretty good."

Mandy looked up from the small, shiny device that looked like a miniature smartphone. "Of course it felt good. He was being a bully. He deserved what he got. If I was back in LA, I'd be posting footage of him in the fountain all over social media." She waved her device. "As it is, I can just complain to Dorn."

Serge hid behind his arm again. "What will the High

Command say when they hear about this? We've never had a blot on the tribute bride program like this before."

Bridget hesitated. "Come on. I know you've had Earth women who've declined their matches before."

"Declined, yes," Serge said, holding up a finger. "Tossed into a fountain in front of the entire promenade? No."

Mandy rolled her eyes. "He'll get over it. He shouldn't have grabbed Bridget so hard."

Bridget glanced at the finger-shaped bruises on her arm. Over the past hour they've gone from red to purple, and were tender to the touch. Anger coursed through her when she thought about the big Drexian who'd grabbed her. If it hadn't been for Reina, he might have been able to drag her off. She gave an involuntary shudder at the thought.

"I just hope I'm not removed from the program," Reina said. "I love working with brides." She gave Mandy and Bridget both a smile. "I'm not sorry I pushed him, though."

"Who would have thought I'd go down like this?" Serge wailed.

Mandy's fingers flew across the surface of her device. "Dorn won't let that happen."

Reina nodded, but didn't look convinced. Bridget folded a blouse and laid it inside the suitcase then walked back over to the dresser. She paused and put a hand on Reina's arm. "We won't let that happen."

"You should be given a medal for defending Bridget," Mandy said. "Isn't your job to take care of us?"

Reina pulled herself up to her full, and quite impressive, height. "You're right. It is my job to take care of tribute brides."

"Then you were just doing your job," Bridget said giving her a wink. "Very well, I might add."

Two pink spots appeared on Reina's light-gray cheeks.

"What now?" Serge asked, peeking one eye out from

underneath his arm. "I suppose if the wedding is officially off I shouldn't even be here. If we aren't fired, Reina and I will probably be assigned to a new tribute bride." He let out a tortured sigh. "I can only hope she's got the figure you do."

Reina looked at him and made a *tsk*-ing noise in the back of her throat, disappearing into the bathroom and returning moments later with a wet towel. She slapped it onto Serge's forehead, and he gave a high-pitched yelp.

"It's a cold compress," she said. "It should help you cool off."

More muttering came from Serge, but he adjusted the towel over his head. "I don't suppose there's anyway to talk you into reconciliation?"

Bridget pulled an armful of dresses out of the wardrobe and dropped them into the suitcase. "With that guy? Not a chance."

"What about another match?" Reina asked.

Bridget shook her head. "No more matches."

"But you'll have to go to the other side of the station," Reina said, beginning to wring her hands again. She lowered her voice. "With the other tribute brides who rejected their mates."

"It can't be that bad," Bridget said as she looked at the stricken expression on the Vexling's face.

"I've never been there," Reina admitted.

"You're not going to go over there," Mandy said, her eyes glued to her device. "I'm lodging a formal protest with the High Command. Karsh's bad behavior means you should get an exemption from the rules. You should be allowed to stay on this side of the station with the rest of us."

Bridget smiled and felt warmed by her friend's fierce defense. "I'm sure I'll be fine there. If there are other Earth women, it can't be so bad."

"Absolutely not," Mandy said, her face flushed. "Why should you be punished because your so-called fiancé doesn't know how to treat women? And you can stop packing. I'm telling you, there's no way I'm going to let them kick you out because of the way that brute behaved. It's his fault, not yours. Time's up, Drexians."

"Not all Drexians are like Karsh," Reina said.

"Oh, I know." Bridget thought of Kax, and her pulse quickened.

"Then why not consider another match?" Reina asked.

"Because I'm already in love with a Drexian who doesn't want me." Bridget felt the words rush out of her.

Serge sat bolt upright, and his cold compress slipped off his head and landed on the floor with a smack. Reina spun and stared at Bridget with her mouth agape, while Mandy looked up from her device.

"With a Drexian?" Serge asked.

Reina blinked hard. "And he doesn't want you?"

Bridget nodded and looked away before she started crying.

"Kax?" Reina's voice was barely a whisper.

Bridget didn't look up, but didn't deny it, either.

Serge sucked in a breath so loudly Bridget thought he might be on the verge of hyperventilating. "You're in love with Dorn's brother? When did this happen?" He waved his hands. "Don't tell me. When you were marooned on that mining colony, right?"

Reina pressed her spindly fingers to her cheeks. "You fell in love while you were stranded? How romantic!"

Bridget shook her head. "I told you. He doesn't want me. Not in that way at least."

"Not true." The deep voice from the doorway made everyone jump. "I do want you. In every way."

Bridget's heart leapt as she recognized Kax's voice.

He walked into the room and everyone stared at him, including Bridget, who felt like she was looking at a mirage. "I thought you were on a mission."

"I'm back," he said. "Are you okay?"

She bobbed her head up and down, noticing Mandy wave Reina and Serge out of the room with her.

Bridget took in the smudges on his face, and the scorch marks on his uniform. He looked like he'd come down a chimney and smelled like burnt hair. "I think I should be asking if you're okay."

He glanced down at his singed uniform, as if seeing it for the first time. "I'm fine." He stepped closer. "You rejected the match?"

"I had to," Bridget said. "It wouldn't have been fair to marry him when I'm in love with someone else."

Kax closed the distance between them with two long steps, pulling her into his arms and holding her tightly as he leaned down. "I thought you didn't believe in love."

"And I thought you didn't want me," Bridget said, her voice cracking. "You told me we couldn't be together."

Kax held her tighter. "I only said that to protect you." He closed his eyes as he forced the words from his mouth. "I was exposed to radiation during an undercover mission years ago. The doctors think the chances of me fathering children are slim."

Bridget squeezed him, feeling the hard planes of his muscles against her cheek. "I don't care about that. All I care about is being with you."

"Really?" Kax said. "I thought every woman wanted children."

Bridget shrugged. "The doctor said the chances were slim, not impossible, right?"

He let a small laugh escape. "I guess so."

"Then I'll take those odds," Bridget said. "I've never listened to people who said I couldn't do something, anyway. And I know we'll have fun trying."

"Are you positive?" Kax asked. "Drexians mate for life. That is, if the High Command will even allow it."

"I've never been more sure about anything," Bridget gazed up at him, locking onto his eyes while she wrapped her arms around him and rubbed her fingers along his nodes. "And after the scene I pulled with Karsh, I'm sure the High Command will be thrilled to get me off their hands."

"Cinnara," he murmured, as he lowered his mouth to hers and his nodes became hard beneath her touch. She'd heard Mandy's mate call her 'cinnara,' and knew it was a Drexian term of endearment. Bridget had never been one for pet names, but she felt a rush of both pleasure and tenderness at hearing the word. Kax kissed her deeply, and her tender feelings deepened into a burning desire. When he finally released her, she felt lightheaded.

"I guess we should tell Serge the good news," Kax said.

Bridget gave him a questioning look.

Kax ran a finger down the side of her cheek. "He's got a wedding to start planning."

Bridget slid one hand from his back to his chest, and then to his taut stomach muscles before finally reaching the hard bulge in his pants. She rubbed against his cock and licked her lips. "Serge can wait."

CHAPTER
THIRTY-TWO

Kax looked up at the wood-beamed ceiling, and adjusted his head on one of the faux-fur pillows. He'd thrown off the thick, chocolate-brown duvet, as well as the ivory cashmere throw, from the end of the bed, and they lay in a pile next to the king-size mahogany sleigh bed.

He turned his head to one side, spotting the fireplace against one wall and a sliding glass door leading out onto a snow-dusted balcony. "This fantasy suite is very different from Mandy's."

Bridget pushed herself up on her elbows, and the sheet fell off her bare back. Her hair was tousled and her cheeks flushed, and a pretty sheen of sweat glistened on her chest. "You're just noticing this now?" She swatted playfully at him. "I'm in the Swiss Alps wing, and she's in the South Pacific wing."

Kax rolled her over onto her back and hovered over her, watching her pupils dilate as his hard, naked body pressed against hers. "I was a little busy up until now."

She bit her bottom lip. "Too busy to notice where you were?"

He lowered his mouth to her neck and nipped, moving his bites down until he reached her nipples, which were pebbled. "Much too busy." He took one in his mouth and rolled his tongue around it, feeling her breath hitch in her chest. "But now, I'd like to take my time."

Bridget arched her back as he sucked harder, tugging it gently between his teeth before moving to the next one and lavishing attention on it until her breath quickened.

"I couldn't hold back before," he said as he slid down, kissing her belly as he went. "I needed to know you're mine."

"I'm all yours," she said, her voice breathy as his stubble tickled her inner thighs. "You know that."

He spread her legs gently and moaned at the sight of her. He parted her with his tongue, dragging it slowly and swirling it around her swollen nub, enjoying the feel of her shuddering beneath him. His cock throbbed with desire, but he wanted to focus on her pleasure. She was his, every gorgeous bit of her, and he would never lose her again. He reached his hands under her round ass and lifted her hips up, opening her wider to him.

"So beautiful, cinnara," he whispered. He couldn't imagine a more perfect female, and still couldn't believe she wanted him. He flicked and sucked her slick nub until she trembled, her hands clawing at the sheets. He loved the sweet taste of her; the soft scent of her skin; and the intoxicating feel of her curves.

"I'm almost there," she gasped.

"I know." He lifted his head for a moment and met her eyes as he slid one thick finger inside her. "I want to feel you come."

She rolled her head back and her muscles clenched his finger as she cried out his name. Kax eased another finger in, feeling her stretch and spasm at the same time. He lowered his mouth and blew, causing her to bolt up and wrap her legs around his shoulders.

"Kax!" She screamed and thrashed on the bed until her shaking dissolved into faint tremors, and her legs sagged against him.

He let her collapse onto the bed and climbed up, kissing her lazily as he went until he covered her body with his own. Her eyes were heavy with desire as she hooked one leg around his waist.

"I want more," she whispered, running her tongue along her bottom lip.

He closed his own eyes for a moment to regain control. His rock-hard cock pressed against her thigh, but he wanted to go slow. "Has anyone ever told you you're a temptress?"

She gave him a wicked grin. "I'm only tempting you with what's already yours."

He bent his head and buried it in her neck, inhaling the warmth of her skin, and feeling a jolt as she arched her back and her breasts rubbed against him. He pushed the crown of his cock into her and held it steady, feeling her tightness as he leaned back and met her hot, liquid gaze.

"Who's the tease now?" She reached her arms around and dug her fingers into his ass, dropping her voice to a dark purr. "I want every inch of that cock inside me, tough guy."

Her words arrowed through him, blinding him with need. He couldn't hold back any longer, and he thrust into her, stroking deep as her hands dug into his flesh. Her heat enveloped him, as he plunged into her again and again, his moans blending with hers.

"I love the way you fill me," she said, her voice hoarse and her hands pulling him deeper into her.

He sat back, grasping her hips and holding her up, the new angle making her eyes widen as he buried his cock to the hilt.

He looked down where their bodies were joined. "Love watching you stretch so tight for me."

Her gaze followed his, and she smiled as he dragged his thick cock out and thrust it back in. He loved how she watched him take her, her eyelids flickering with each deep stroke.

"Sweet talker," she said, arching her hips up, wanting even more.

He reached down and circled a thumb over her slick bundle of nerves as he powered into her, watching the pleasure on her face as her heat clamped around him, her release rippling through her. He held her tight and savored every pulse, feeling his own orgasm building. He made a raw sound as it tore through him and he reared back, feeling nothing but her exquisite grip on his cock as he exploded with one final hard thrust. He gave a final, contented growl as he sank onto the bed beside her, breathing heavily.

Bridget rolled on top of him and rested her head on his chest. "It sounds like you ran a marathon."

"I don't know what a marathon is, but if it makes you feel like your heart will explode, then yes. I have run one of those."

"I don't want to wear you out." Her voice teased him. "I'm sure we could ease off a bit next time."

His hand slid up into her hair. "Only if you feel you cannot handle all of me."

She traced her fingers down the corded muscles of his stomach. "Oh, I can handle all of you." She lifted her head to smile at him as her fingers wandered lower. "You know I love taking every delicious inch of you."

He felt a flush of heat in his core. "At this rate, we'll never leave your suite again."

"Fine by me," she said, her voice wavering. "I don't ever want to lose the feeling I have with you here, right now."

He captured her face in his hand. "You will never lose me. I promise." He pulled her gaze to his. "It's you and me together from here on out. No matter what."

She nodded. "No matter what."

The feeling of possessing her heart was even more exhilarating than the feeling of possessing her body. He slid her up so he could kiss her, her full lips soft and sweet against his. When he pulled back, her eyes were filled with tears. He brushed them away with his thumbs.

"This is all new to me," she said. "This love thing can feel a little overwhelming."

"We'll take it slow, cinnara," he said.

She raised an eyebrow.

"Okay, maybe not slow." He brushed a strand of hair off her face. "But I promise you won't have to do anything you don't want to do. We don't even have to have a wedding, if you don't want to."

She slapped his chest. "Oh, I'm definitely marrying you."

He pulled her tighter, his throat making it hard for him to speak.

"I would never break Serge's heart by denying him that," Bridget said.

Kax swatted her bare ass. "You're worrying about Serge's heart?" He lifted her hips so she hovered over his hard cock, and she twitched her ass as her eyes sparkled with challenge. "It looks like my work here isn't done."

CHAPTER
THIRTY-THREE

"I'm still not sure why you insisted on these prickly things in the bouquets." Serge flinched as he rearranged his grasp on the two clusters of white roses and amaryllis.

"It's called holly," Bridget said, brushing the veil off her shoulder. "It goes with the theme of the wedding."

"Which I still don't understand," Serge muttered. "Why have a wedding in the cold, when there's a perfectly lovely waterfront gazebo available? Even the overdone butterfly garden would have been better than this."

"Hey," Mandy said, as she adjusted the spaghetti strap of her claret-colored sequined bridesmaid dress. "I got married in the butterfly garden."

Serge's perfectly arched eyebrows popped up a few centimeters. "And it was perfection, darling." He shivered and made a face. "This..."

"Is a Christmas wedding," Bridget said. "It's my favorite holiday, and I always loved the wedding scene in *Love, Actually*."

"No chance we could throw on a sweater, is there?" Trista asked, holding her bridesmaid bouquet in one hand and rubbing her arm briskly with the other.

Bridget smiled at her. "You can wear what you want after the ceremony."

Serge swung his gaze toward Trista. "That does not mean changing into pants."

As Trista mumbled something about despots, Mandy touched a finger to the feathers at the neckline of Bridget's tulle wedding gown. "Monti and Randi did a great job recreating the dress, but I never pegged you for a sappy-movie type of girl."

"We all have our guilty pleasures," Bridget said, her heels crunching in the holographic snow.

She peeked around the wall of the sheer netting to get a glimpse of the ceremony set up, and her breath hitched in her chest. It was exactly as she'd imagined it. A circle of tall birch trees stood at the end of a snow-covered aisle, their bare branches up lit with white light. Lanterns were positioned at the ends of each row of chairs, and the candles inside them glowed, as shimmering flakes fell softly from the sky. It wasn't overly decorated, and it definitely wasn't anything Serge would consider fabulous, but it was simple and starkly beautiful, and she loved it.

"Speaking of guilty pleasures," Mandy said. "Here comes mine."

Dorn strode up to them in his full military uniform, his dark hair brushed back. He nodded at Bridget and Trista before looking at his mate like he wanted to devour her.

Mandy grinned at him and spun around in her floor-length gown. "You like the dress?"

He slid a finger under one of the thin straps and made a

deep, guttural noise. "I would prefer to see it in a pile on the floor."

Serge cleared his throat. "Do I need to remind you who's wedding this is, and also what happened the last time you two couldn't keep your hands off each other?"

Dorn's gaze dropped to the floor, and Mandy blushed.

"Don't make them feel bad," Bridget said. "That was no one's fault but the Kronock. Anyway, if I hadn't been abducted, Kax wouldn't have come after me, and we may have never fallen in love."

"I never thought of it like that," Mandy said, letting out a breath. "That makes me feel so much better."

Dorn cocked an eyebrow at her. "How much better?"

She gave him a small push. "Not *that* much better. Aren't you supposed to be with the groom, anyway?"

Dorn laughed. "You see how bossy she is with me?"

"Turnabout's fair play." Mandy winked at him. "I still owe you big time, buddy."

Dorn backed away, and Bridget pretended to fan herself. "I'm glad to see things haven't cooled down between you two."

"Drexian men are full of surprises," Mandy said. "The biggest one being Dorn arranging for me to intern in the medical bay."

"I'm so glad you're working there." Bridget squeezed her hand. "I knew you were a natural when I saw you take care of Dorn's injuries."

"It's something I've always wanted to learn more about, but society girls in LA don't become nurses or paramedics," Mandy said, blinking away tears. "Here, I can be."

Trista and Bridget both put an arm around her as Serge scolded them not to mess up their makeup.

"First, Reina gets to update the tribute bride program, and now you get something cool to do," Bridget said.

Serge almost dropped the bouquets. "Reina's doing what?"

"Don't worry," Mandy said, with a wave of her hand toward Serge. "She's not muscling in on your job. She's just updating some of their designs. The 70s influence has got to go."

Her eyes drifted to Serge's forest-green velvet suit with flared lapels and gold piping.

"What?" he asked. "Monti and Randi said this suit would be perfect for a winter wedding."

Bridget squeezed his hand. "I think you look nice."

Serge sniffed. "One does try."

"I don't mind the 70s," Trista said. "I still think Farah Fawcett had the best hair."

Mandy appraised the blonde, tapping one polished fingernail on her chin. "You could pull off Farah Fawcett hair."

"Could we please focus?" Serge rolled his eyes as he shook his head.

Reina hurried up, her blue hair blending perfectly with the frosty setting. "Kax is ready. As soon as the music starts, we can send you down the aisle."

Bridget's stomach fluttered as the sounds of a flute playing "Have Yourself a Merry Little Christmas" wafted down the aisle. Serge thrust a bouquet in her hand, and Reina picked up Bridget's train and unfurled it behind her.

Mandy gave her hand a squeeze. "Remember, just say yes to everything they ask you." She stepped forward as Serge motioned for her to begin walking behind Trista. "I'll see you down there."

Bridget concentrated on taking deep, steady breaths. There was no reason to be nervous. She was marrying the guy she was head-over-heels in love with. They'd both convinced the High Command she wouldn't marry anyone but him, and had gotten approval for their wedding *and* to stay in Bridget's fantasy suite. Everything had worked out perfectly.

Sure, Karsh hadn't been happy, but he'd left the station to take command of a ship far away from Earth and close to several pleasure planets, so Bridget figured he'd get over the whole thing pretty quickly.

Kax had even gotten special permission to delay his next mission until after their wedding and honeymoon. She felt her insides warm at the thought of spending the next few days curled up next to Kax. Even though she'd never imagined she'd live on an alien space station with holographic oceans and chalets perched on fake mountains, there was no place she'd rather be.

Serge waved her forward and she felt Reina straighten her veil. As she stepped around the sheer divider, she spotted Kax standing at the end of the aisle under the illuminated tree branches. His hair was spiked up, and he sported the faint stubble she found so sexy. He smiled when he saw her, his green eyes shining with what she suspected might be tears. He blinked a few times and straightened his broad shoulders, the sash across his military uniform pulling taut.

Bridget knew she should be thinking about the solemn promises she was about to make, but the only thought going through her mind was how fast she could get him out of his uniform. She winked at him, her tongue wetting her bottom lip, and saw his pupils dilate. Being married to a Drexian warrior was going to be fun.

EPILOGUE

Krav attempted to push the rubble off his legs as sirens screamed overhead. The air was filled with the acrid smell of burning, and he coughed as it seared his throat.

"Commander!" The voice sounded far away even though he saw the soldier leaning over him. "Commander Krav, we're going to get you out of here."

Krav let his gaze shift from the soldier's face to the torn ceiling overhead. The explosion had blasted a hole in the building and brought down part of the floor above him. Metal beams and wires hung down from the gaping hole, and black blood splattered what remained of the walls.

The last thing Krav remembered was seeing *that* Drexian only moments before the bomb detonated. The one who'd taken his female and ruined his plans. Anger surged through him, but was dampened by sharp pain as he attempted to move.

He looked down to where Kronock soldiers were trying to remove a fragment of a metal beam from across his legs. As they lifted it, black fluid gushed from his thighs and his vision blurred.

"Vos," he called, hearing the weakness in his own voice and gritting his teeth. "Where is Vos?"

"I am here, Commander."

Although it was covered in dust and smeared with red, Krav let out a long breath when he saw the familiar face. He reached for the soldier's hand, pulling him close. "You must finish what I started."

"You will finish it yourself, Commander."

Krav gave a rough shake of his head. "I will not, but you will." He gripped the hand tightly. "You *must*. Remember what I taught you. Remember my plan. *Our* plan."

"Find a human female," Vos said, his voice flat, as if he'd repeated these things many times. "Take from her what we did not get from the other one. Make her Kronock. Then make all the humans Kronock."

"Yes." Krav was pleased to hear his own words echoed back to him. He locked eyes with the soldier above him. "If we destroy the humans, we destroy the Drexians."

Vos flinched. "Yes, Krav."

As the Kronock commander felt the blood pumping out of him and the screams in the background faded, he hoped he'd been right about Vos. He'd put so much into the soldier—so much training, so much trust, so much hope.

"You will not be alone," he said, spitting out the words through the pain. "Remember the ones on the inside. They are key to our plan."

Vos was also a key to Krav's master plan. It wasn't enough to bring down his enemy. Krav believed a war strategy should have a certain poetic justice. He swallowed, tasting the bitter tang of his own blood, and looked into the turquoise blue eyes of his protégé.

Krav wished he could see his enemy's reaction. To be destroyed by one of their own? How sweet it would be, he thought, as he breathed out for the last time, a grin twisting his thin, gray lips.

THANK YOU FOR READING SEIZED! If you enjoyed this alien abduction romance, you'll love EXPOSED. Katie's life as a paparazzo in LA was circling the drain. And that was *before* she was abducted from Earth as a tribute bride. To make matters worse? Her Drexian warrior fiancé is hiding a dark past that could keep them apart forever.

One-click EXPOSED Now>

"My oh my! Talk about steamy love scenes with high-octane action blended perfectly!"-Amazon Reviewer

Thank you for reading!
This book has been edited and proofed, but typos are like little gremlins that like to sneak in when we're not looking. If you spot a typo, please report it to: tana@tanastone.com
Thank you!!

SNEAK PEEK OF EXPOSED—BOOK 3 IN THE TRIBUTE BRIDES OF THE DREXIAN WARRIORS SERIES

Chapter One

Zayn worked the chains fastened around his wrists, feeling the weak spot he'd made over the past few weeks with a loose shard of steel. Just a little more and he'd be free, he thought, straining against the metal and pushing the pain aside. Blood trickled down his wrist, but he ignored the sharp tang that hit his nose. It wasn't worse than anything else he'd smelled since being thrown into the dungeon over a month ago.

He glanced around the dank cell that held nothing more than a cot and a metal bucket. Considering how technologically advanced his enemy was, Zayn had been surprised to find their prison so rudimentary. Of course, he hadn't known just how advanced the Kronock had become until he'd been taken captive.

He let out a low growl and the rusted metal walls echoed it back to him. Being captured had not been part of the plan. As a member of the Drexian military team sent to defend a research colony near enemy space, his mission had been to repel the

Kronock and destroy their ships. That hadn't worked out so well when his entire team had been slaughtered by an enemy considerably more sophisticated than they'd suspected. Well, not the entire team. Him, they'd kept alive.

He tried not to think about the surprise attack that had left the other warriors dead and had landed him inside a Kronock prison. His people hadn't ventured into enemy territory in decades, battling their crude and brutish foes on the borders of Kronock space and repelling the would-be invaders on the outskirts of the solar system the Drexians protected. They had no need. The Kronock were predictable in their attacks, but they were outmatched by Drexian technology and warfare. Had been since they first attempted to invade Earth over thirty years earlier. Or so his people had thought.

Zayn's blood heated as he flashed back to how easily the Kronock had disabled their weapons, the efficient way the gray-scaled creatures had slaughtered his comrades, and the sophisticated ship they'd dragged him onto, bloody and broken. It was clear to him now that the enemy had spent years lying low and pretending to be oafish brutes, all the while developing technology to blow the Drexians—and Earthlings—out of the sky.

The only thing they hadn't changed was how they tortured captives. That had been old school. A sharp pain pierced his side as he breathed in too quickly, and he knew he had at least one broken rib. The skin on his arms had stopped healing from the lashes he'd taken with a laser whip, the gashes deep and oozing. He shook off the discomfort. They would heal once he was away from the daily abuse, as would the skin on his wrist he was scraping off as he loosened his chains. The crucial thing was getting off the ship and back to his people so he could tell them what he'd learned.

Zayn tugged at his wrists and felt the metal give, finally

snapping and clattering to the floor. He paused to listen for the rush of feet, but there was nothing. He touched his raw flesh, grateful to be free of the shackles and the burden of dragging the heavy chain with him when he moved. Shaking his hands to regain some of the feeling, he ran them through his hair. It had become shaggy and matted in the weeks or months he'd been held—he'd lost all track of time in the dark cell—and his fingers tangled in the dark locks.

"Time to have another chat with the General," a voice said, from the end of the corridor.

His auditory implant made is easy for him to understand the guttural words of his enemy, but still, the rough sounds grated on his nerves.

Zayn reluctantly picked up the chains again and held them around his wrists, flinching from the contact and hoping his jailor wouldn't notice the broken clasp. He didn't respond to the Kronock. He never did. He never said a word, a tactic that had earned him more electric shocks than he could count, and beatings so severe he usually blacked out and had to be carried back to his cell. The worst had been when they'd electrified the bumpy nodes running along the length of his spine. Normally an indicator of arousal, they were sensitive to touch, and he'd writhed in pain each time they'd sent a jolt through them.

A tall alien approached the door, his wide, clawed feet tapping on the floor and announcing his arrival before his bald, scaled head appeared in the window. He looked at Zayn through the metal panel grafted to his eye socket, and the red, bionic eye flashed as it scanned him. Zayn had learned that aside from being huge and strong, some of the Kronock had augmented themselves with technology, the bionic eyes being the most obvious addition. He knew there was more he couldn't see beneath the armor grafted to their scales, which was why they'd been able to overpower him and his team.

Zayn swallowed the taste of bile as he thought of how outmatched they'd been. That was why he would need to be faster and smarter to make it out alive.

As the door creaked open, Zayn took a breath. *This is it,* he thought. *Now or never.*

The Kronock stepped inside to take him by the arm as he usually did, but at the last moment Zayn feinted to one side, rolling his shoulder and spinning around, before whipping the chains around the jailor's head and darting for the door. Stunned, it took the Kronock a moment to react, and by that time, Zayn had slammed the door shut behind him and locked him in.

Zayn didn't stop to listen for the roar of frustration. He was already halfway down the corridor, when he heard a noise to his left and swung his head toward one of the cell doors. The noise wasn't the harsh language of the Kronock. It was the Drexian language. It might have been weeks or months since he'd heard it spoken anywhere but in his own head, but he knew the sound of his own tongue.

He glanced through the window cut into the door and saw a bare, muscular back hunched over in the corner, the bronze skin and raised nodes confirming his initial guess. This was a Drexian.

"Brother," he called out. "Come with me."

The man raised his head but didn't turn. "You're Drexian?"

"Yes," Zayn said, impatient to get away but not willing to leave another warrior behind. "I'm getting out of here, and you're coming with me."

The Drexian shook his head. "Impossible. Go without me."

"I can get you out," Zayn said, leaning against the metal bars and being startled when the door swung open.

The Drexian prisoner stood, his hands in tight fists by his side. "It's too late for me. Go before they come for you."

Zayn started to shake his head when the other prisoner turned and focused his red, bionic eye on him. "They've made me one of them. I can't go back after what they've done to me. After what they've put inside my head." His arms shook as he spoke. "Even now, I have an urge to kill you."

Zayn backed away, his throat constricting and making it difficult to speak.

"Go," the Drexian hybrid strode forward and pushed the door shut. "Save yourself."

Zayn stumbled away, his eyes not leaving the cell door that had not been locked.

"Wait," the Drexian called after him.

Zayn met his eyes.

"The next time you see me." The red eye blinked as he spoke. "Do not hesitate to kill me."

Zayn didn't answer, his gut twisting in a knot as he continued down the hall. The guard station was empty, but the metal wall cabinet that held extra weapons was not. He ripped the cabinet door off its hinges and grabbed two blasters from inside. He guessed he had no more than a minute before his escape was detected, so he needed to move fast. He pushed the thought of the other Drexian warrior out of his mind. If he let the feelings of rage and regret fill him, he would not be able to do what he needed to do.

Running down another narrow hallway, Zayn ducked into a closet as he heard footsteps pounding toward him. He'd learned what he knew about the ship by feigning unconsciousness when he was dragged back and forth from being tortured. Sometimes his eyes really had been swollen shut, but other times he'd only pretended to be half dead. If his memory served him, the shuttle bays and flight decks were one level up. He glanced above him, breathing a sigh of relief when he saw a vent covering.

Zayn clambered up into the ceiling and pulled the covering back into place. Crawling as quietly as he could, he followed the vents up, using his elbows and knees to gain traction in the tubes. When he was sure he'd reached the right level, he slid a panel back and dipped his head down.

The dim corridor was empty, so he lowered himself, holding on with one hand as he slid the ceiling panel back into place before landing on the floor with a thud. He kept close to the wall as he hurried toward a wide door, which slid open as soon as he stood in front of it.

"You're going to make it," he whispered to himself as he took in the expansive flight deck.

Ducking out of sight behind a stack of metal barrels, he eyed the array of ships. He needed to find one that was leaving as soon as possible, and one big enough on which to stow away. That eliminated the shiny, two-seater fighters, and the cargo ships still loading up. His gaze lingered on a rusted, banged-up ship, and he watched a squat alien pilot stride on board, rolls of dark purple flesh jiggling as he walked.

"A scavenger," he said, rubbing his hands together. He recognized the rotund alien as a trader of space junk. It wasn't the fastest ship, or the best smelling, but it would probably get the least amount of scrutiny.

Edging his way around the flight deck by darting between crates and containers, he dashed up the ship's ramp as it began to lift and rolled into the ship. As he watched the ramp slam shut behind him, he flinched. After being the only member of his team to survive, he was now leaving a Drexian behind. Not really a Drexian anymore, he reminded himself, taking a breath and trying not to think of the metal eye implant grafted into his kinsman's flesh.

He looked around the quiet ship and guessed the captain was busy piloting, so he crept to the rear, slipping into a particularly dirty bathroom just big enough for him to close the door while holding his breath.

Zayn felt the ship begin to move, then accelerate, and when he felt the jump to light speed he let his shoulders relax long enough to shift the grip on his blaster. He stepped out and cracked his neck by twisting it from side to side. "Time to talk to the pilot about setting a new course."

Chapter Two

Katie walked along Rodeo Drive, her camera tucked into a pink leather bag slung over her shoulder as she scouted the sidewalk looking for celebrities. She tried to look casual as she peered into the storefronts, but she was a bundle of nerves. It didn't help that it was a thousand degrees, and she'd had to cover her hair with a scarf.

"Come on," she muttered to herself. "There has to be a Hilton heiress out shopping today. Or a Kardashian. I *need* something."

A thin woman carrying a beige Birkin bag gave her a sideways glance. Katie sized her up as no one worth photographing and gave her what she hoped was her most innocent smile. The woman wasn't fooled and moved away, shooting a nasty look over her shoulder.

This was a disaster. She knew her desperation was palpable, which was the kiss of death in her business. Even though she was tall, with striking red hair and more curves than were typically accepted in LA, she'd always had the confidence to blend in anywhere. It probably came from growing up with a father who was a grifter and had taught her everything from three card Monte to how to work a mark. It wasn't tough to see that he was why she'd ended up as a paparazzo for some of the top Internet gossip sites.

"I just need one shot," she said, more to bolster her confidence than anything. "Just one great shot to get me through this."

This meant the disaster that had become her life since she'd taken the last known photo of the socialite Mandy Talbot before she disappeared. Katie closed her eyes briefly, willing herself to go back in time and *not* take that image of Mandy outside of the restaurant after her best friend and TV starlet London had left their standing lunch date.

At the time, Katie had thought it was gold. Mandy was cleared distraught in the image, and the headline the tabloid rag ran next to it proclaimed the TV producer's daughter to be an "Instagram diva ditched by best friend and boyfriend." It had netted Katie a tidy sum, enough to cover rent, since her stand-up-comedian boyfriend hadn't gotten a gig in weeks. It had also been the last image anyone could find of the woman who had apparently vanished the day the photo was taken.

Katie had been interviewed by the police, and by the private investigators hired by Mandy's dad. Somehow, those investigators had been able to dig into her financial life and see the debt she was in. That was all they needed to decide she was somehow involved in the disappearance, and it had all been downhill from there. She'd ended up on the pages of the very magazines she usually shot for, headlines proclaiming her as the last person to see the heiress alive and painting a picture of her as someone with nothing to lose.

She adjusted her oversized sunglasses. Part of her was glad her father hadn't lived to see this. She was supposed to be the one hunting for celebrities trying to blend in or avoid detection, not the one hiding. Not that she'd been shocked when her fellow paparazzi had turned on her. No honor among thieves, and all that.

"Katie!" A voice from across the street made her jump and turn before she could stop herself. She heard a click of a shutter.

She cursed at herself. "Dammit, you know better."

She started walking briskly in the other direction, dodging people and trying to put distance between herself and the photographer. She thought it might be that weasely guy from the *Enquirer*, but no way was she going to turn around to check. Figures, she thought. Only the bottom feeders were still hounding her after all these weeks.

"Where's Mandy?" the voice yelled after her.

At this point, people were staring and beginning to recognize her. She kept her head down and held her bag tight, barely avoiding a run-in with one of the Schwarzenegger kids. Shit, she should have been taking his photo, not trying to avoid flattening him while she made a run for it.

She ducked around the corner and nearly ran the two blocks to where she'd parked her piece-of-shit car. Jumping in, she tossed her bag on the passenger seat and floored it, looking in the rearview mirror once she was moving. No one behind her, that was good. But she hadn't gotten a single photo. That was bad.

It took her almost an hour to reach her apartment in the Valley, which gave Katie plenty of time to think about just how badly her life was falling apart, since her car's radio wasn't working.

"Think," she told herself, letting the wind from the open window cool her. "What would dad do?"

He'd managed to get himself out of plenty of scrapes over the years, and he'd usually been guilty as hell. How had she managed to get herself in such a big mess without having done anything wrong?

The problem was the TV producer dad and his rabid dog investigators. They seemed hell-bent on blaming the girl's disappearance on someone, and didn't seem to be too concerned about the details. Katie had thought the dad was faking it the first time he'd appeared on the news with his collagen-enhanced third wife. She knew a faker when she saw one, and that guy didn't give a shit about finding his daughter. He wanted people to think he did, though. Hence the private investigators eager to find a fall guy.

Katie pulled up in front of her apartment building and the car shuddered to a stop. She rubbed her fingers on the steering wheel and whispered to the car, "I just need you to hold out a little bit longer. I really can't take one more thing going wrong right now."

What she needed was to provide an ironclad alibi to the police and have them call off the investigators. And the best way to do that was to enlist the help of her boyfriend. He may not be great when it came to making money, but she knew he had her back when it mattered. At least she thought he did.

Katie took the stairs to her third-floor, garden apartment two at a time, waving at an elderly neighbor, who clearly didn't read tabloid news since she smiled brightly. She opened her front door and called out as she walked inside.

"Mark, I need your help—" The words died on her lips as she stood in the near-empty living room, looking at a faded couch and an empty TV stand.

The flat screen was gone, along with the contents of the bookshelf and the framed prints on the wall, leaving metal hooks to dangle at eye level. Her mouth went dry and she dropped her bag and keys on the floor.

No, this wasn't happening. It couldn't be happening. How had they been robbed? Mark was supposed to be home all day.

"Mark?" She went into the bedroom, and saw that her laptop was gone from her desk. She opened the closet and her heart tightened. Where her boyfriend's clothes had been were only a few wire hangers, but her clothes were all still there. They hadn't been robbed. Mark had left. "And that bastard took my computer."

She pulled her cell phone from her pocket and dialed his number as she stomped back into the living room. She didn't mind his leaving, nearly as much as she minded him taking everything of value in the apartment. The asshole hadn't even paid for any of it.

Her call went straight to voicemail. Typical. She doubted he'd be answering any of her calls from now on. She left him a colorful message telling him exactly what she thought of him, then threw the phone onto the carpeted floor, sinking down next to it and letting her head fall into her hands.

After a moment, she straightened up. Mark had been right, even if she hated him for being the first one to think of it. She had to get out of there. She didn't have money for rent, and that was due in less than a week. She couldn't make money with every paparazzi in town angling for a photo of her. She needed to get out of town before it was too late.

She hurried back to the bedroom, reaching under the bed for her suitcase. Nothing. The asshole had even taken her suitcase.

"You have got to be shitting me," she screamed, then took a deep breath and tried to shake it off. It was fine. She'd just have to pile her clothes onto the back seat of her car.

She grabbed an armful of shirts from the closet and headed for the front door, stopping and nearly dropping the pile when she saw the man standing in the doorway. If she wasn't already so upset, alarm bells would have been going off in the back of her head. As it was, she was too irritated to be afraid, even though the man had to be almost seven feet tall and built like a linebacker.

"Can I help you?"

He wore sunglasses so she couldn't see his eyes, but he pivoted his head to take in the shabby surroundings. "I believe it will be the other way around."

To be continued . . .

To read more of EXPOSED, Zayn and Katie's story, and Book 3 in the Tribute Brides of the Drexian Warriors series, click HERE!

Get this free bonus content by clicking below (but I suggest you read TAMED before reading the bonus wedding story)!

BookHip.com/CRJHNH

PREVIEW OF BOUNTY—BARBARIANS OF THE SAND PLANET #1

Below is a sample of another Tana Stone sci-fi-romance series—this one with alien barbarians and female bounty hunters!

Chapter One

"Are they shooting at us?" Danica asked, grabbing the edge of a smooth, metal console as she stepped onto the bridge and the ship heaved to one side. She tasted blood as she bit the inside of her mouth, and flinched from the pain. *Son of a bitch.*

She and Bexli had just brought their latest captive onboard, and she'd given the order to take off, hoping the rival bounty hunters who'd also been in pursuit hadn't seen them. From the staccato sounds of gunfire, she guessed that her plan of slipping out unnoticed was shot to hell.

She took in the familiar sight of the compact bridge—a round, flat panel console in the center of the room with view screens suspended above it, smaller individual consoles forming a half moon around the main one, and a final ring of screened consoles against the circular walls. A long, narrow slit of a window gave them a view out the front of the ship, but had a steel shade they could lower for security. Nearly every part of the room was composed of metal that was long past gleaming, and looked nearly black with age and grime. Wires spilled from underneath most of the consoles, a result of various hacks and patches to keep the aging space ship running. Danica inhaled the scent of burning fuel that seemed to permeate the ship, and felt a rush of affection for the bucket of bolts she'd practically grown up on.

"Looks like it," her pilot, Caro, said turning from one of the smaller consoles where she navigated the ship, her straight, nearly black hair flying behind her as she spun back around. "And we're definitely outgunned."

"Can we outrun them?" Danica asked, as she made her way down to the center console and looked out at the massive ship blocking their escape.

"What we don't have in size or gun power, we make up for in maneuverability," Caro said. "I should be able to get a little extra acceleration from our impulse drives if I boost the—"

“Caro,” Danica said, cutting off the woman before she launched into an overly detailed explanation of their engine.

“Sorry, Captain,” Caro said spinning back around to her console. “On it.”

"I hope you're right," Tori said from where she stood at the weapons console along the wall, her curly, dark hair pulled up in a topknot and held in place with what looked like metal chopsticks with dangerously sharp ends—almost as sharp as her pointy teeth. A row of hard, raised bumps ran above her eyebrows, down along the sides of her face and disappeared into her hairline—a hallmark of the Zevrians—making her look even fiercer than she was. "Because we're running low on weapons."

"How low?" Danica gripped the console with both hands

as the ship jerked to the right and skirted underneath the larger ship.

"How good are you at hand-to-hand combat?" Tori asked, her brown, muscled arms braced against the wall.

Danica had gotten a lot of flak—mostly from her father's old bounty-hunter friends—when she'd brought on the Zevrian as her security chief, but she'd never had a moment's regret for making Tori a part of her team. Especially in situations like these.

"I thought we were supposed to stock up when we were docked at Centuri Twelve," Danica shouted over the roar of the engines firing.

"I would have, if we had anything to buy them with," Tori said as the ship accelerated.

Danica sighed. Her crew had been running on fumes—sometimes literally—for weeks. "I know it's been tight, but once we turn over this bounty, we'll be flush for a while."

"I'm just glad Mourad won't have the satisfaction of beating us." Caro turned to face forward as the force of acceleration pressed her back into her chair. "I hate that guy."

Danica couldn't agree more. The ship shooting at them belonged to a bounty hunter and mercenary named Mourad, who didn't believe in female bounty hunters and didn't believe in playing fair. Not that Danica was against stretching the rules or pushing her luck, but Mourad had no limits on what he and his crew would do to capture a bounty.

He was the one bounty hunter her father had gone out of his way to avoid, because Mourad ignored all the usual professional courtesies and accepted practices. He would double-cross anyone. Instead of tracking down bounties himself, he was known for waiting until another bounty hunter did all the legwork, then he and his band of mercenaries would swoop in and snake the bounty. Just like he was trying to do now.

Over my dead body, Danica thought, as their ship broke through the atmosphere and shot into space, the sky going from hazy yellow to inky blue to black. She thumped the side of the console, mentally thanking the ship for getting her out of yet another scrape.

When her father died, he'd left everything to her, which meant basically his ship. It had just been the three of them for as long as Danica could remember—her and her father and the ship. Different crews had come and gone, but the ship had been the only constant in their lives, aside from each other. She'd thought about selling it, but only for a moment. The old ship was as much a part of her as her father had been, and she couldn't stand the thought of losing both of them.

She knew her father had never wanted her to take over his bounty-hunting business. Truth be told, he never thought it was possible, but after spending a childhood chasing after crooks all over the galaxy, she didn't really know any other life. She was good at tracking people and getting out of scrapes and skirting the law. Her father had taught her well.

Danica shook thoughts of her father out of her head as she glanced at the fuel gauge. "Good work. We should have enough steam to reach the Gendarvian outpost, where we can unload our bounty and get our reward."

Tori crossed the bridge to stand next to her, the chain belt wrapped several times around her waist jingling as she walked. "I wonder what this one did to command such a high price."

Danica shrugged, tucking a loose strand of wavy, blonde hair behind her ear. "It's not our business to wonder why. I can tell you it wasn't for a violent offense. I've never had a bounty put up less of a fight."

"The tracking was the hard part. Dr. Max Dryden did a fucking brilliant job of hiding."

The women turned to see their engineer, Holly, step onto the bridge. While the rest of Danica's crew favored utilitarian clothes that made them look more like their male counterparts —military issue pants, T-shirts, multi-pocketed vests and jackets—the ship's engineer and resident computer whiz wore color and patterns and combined them fearlessly. Red hair spilled over her shoulders and down the skintight, pink-paisley top she'd paired over an equally snug pair of turquoise pants. Her decidedly feminine appearance didn't do a thing to stop her from cursing like a space pirate, which usually startled people who thought her girly looks meant she was all sugar and spice.

"Not good enough to outfox us," Tori said, hand on her hip.

"Luckily for you, I understand the doctor's research and narrowed it down to the few planets that are ideal for that type of scientific study," Holly said. "And then Bexli did her thing."

Bexli was the other non-human in the crew. A Lycithian shape-shifter who excelled at sneaking in and out of otherwise impenetrable places, she was their ace in the hole. Officially, she was their acquisitions officer, but only in the sense that she could acquire any bounty by way of her shape-shifting skills. She was so indispensable, Danica even put up with the pet glurkin that Bexli had insisted on bringing on board.

"Remind me again what type of research," Tori said, then shook her head. "Never mind, I actually don't care."

Holly rolled her eyes at Tori. "The study of a rare mineral only found in a few systems. Word on the astronet is that the doctor has figured out a way to harness its power, which would be fucking amazing."

Caro twisted in her chair to face them. "I'm still not thrilled we're turning over a scientist. Are we sure this is a legit bounty? How many doctors do you know who commit crimes severe enough to command this amount? Should we really be turning in other women? I mean, we're an all female bounty-hunting crew."

Danica frowned, partly at Caro's barrage of questions and partly because she'd had the same thoughts, and had been trying to ignore her inner voice during the entire search. "We don't have the luxury of picking and choosing our bounties. Anyway, if we don't turn the doctor in, someone else will. At least we treat our prisoners well."

"Not that all of them deserve it." Tori pulled up the hem of her black cargo pants to reveal a thin, red scar running up her calf. "We should have put that Daxian smuggler out the airlock."

"Agreed," Bexli said, as she joined the other women on the bridge, a tiny puff of green fur running along beside her. "He was particularly repulsive."

"Is the bounty all settled?" Danica asked.

Bexli nodded, and her iridescent-lavender bob swung at her jawbone. "This one was a breeze. I didn't even have to transform into something terrifying to keep her in line."

She leaned against a console and scooped Pog up in one arm, ruffling its fur and making it emit a low purr. "The Daxian from our last mission only stopped struggling when I morphed into a gorvon."

"Remind me again, what's a gorvon?" Holly asked.

"A particularly gruesome creature from the Daxian's home world." Bexli grinned. "Lots of claws and fangs."

Caro laughed, tightening her high ponytail. "That explains why he soiled his cell."

"At least he kept us in fuel and rations for a month," Danica said, glancing at Tori. "And you gave him a few scars, if I remember correctly."

Tori grinned. "A souvenir from the bounty hunter babes."

"You know I hate that nickname." Danica folded her arms across her chest.

"Babes is better than the other name they call us that also starts with a *b*." Holly leaned against one of the consoles, crossing her long legs at the ankles.

"I don't mind the name so much," Caro said. "At least they're talking about us."

Danica let out a long breath. "They should be talking about us because we've brought in the two highest bounties in the past astro-year, not because we're all women."

Holly patted her on the shoulder. "It's just because we're the first—and so far only—all-female bounty-hunter crew. Once the novelty wears off, or another crew comes along, people will talk about something else."

Danica knew there was truth in Holly's words, but she hated the fact that even though they'd brought in two of the toughest bounties around, the other hunters still didn't respect them. She'd known working in a field known for tough guys wouldn't be easy, but she'd hoped her unorthodox methods and maverick crew would win her respect. So far, they'd only managed to acquire nicknames.

"I say we own it," Tori said, taking one of the pointy chopsticks from her hair and pressing the needle-like point into the pad of her finger. "We know we can do any job the boys can do and, once we bring in this hot-shot doctor, we'll be rolling in enough dough to outfit this ship so we can blast anyone out of the sky. Let them call us babes then."

"Um, guys." Caro's fingers flew across the screen in front of her. "We probably shouldn't count our money quite yet."

Danica jerked her head to the screens above her, slamming her palm against the console when she saw the rival ship closing in on them. "I thought we had enough of a head start to lose them."

"They're faster than I expected for a ship that large," Caro said, maneuvering their ship so that it dipped to the left.

Holly slid onto the floor, landing with a thud. "A little warning next time."

"Sorry," Caro shouted over the sound of weapons fire hitting their hull. "You should probably brace for impact."

A blast shook the ship and alarms began screaming, red lights flashing overhead.

"Was that a torpedo?" Danica asked, shaking her head in disbelief. Was a rival bounty hunter really trying to blow up her ship?

“Shit.” Holly scrambled to her feet, using the nearest console to pull herself toward the door. "I'd better get back to the engine room. If we lose that, we're dead in the water."

“I’ll go make sure the prisoner is okay,” Bexli said, following Holly with Pog tucked under one arm.

The entire ship jolted, and Danica heard the sound of metal scraping against metal. Her skin went cold. "They've clamped on."

Tori's face was grim. "They're boarding us."

"Maybe they'll take the doctor and go," Caro said, although her voice quivered. Danica knew her pilot had been captured more than once when she was a pilot for a resistance movement, and she suspected it hadn’t always been pleasant.

Danica squeezed her hands into fists. "They're not taking our bounty or us." She turned to Tori. "Hold them off as long as you can, but don't get yourself killed. I have a plan."

Tori pulled the other chopstick from her hair and slipped both sharp metal sticks into her chain belt. "You got it, Captain."

Danica ran off the bridge and down the dimly lit corridor until she reached a steel door where Bexli stood guard. “I’ve got the doctor. Why don't you and Pog try to hold off Mourad's soldiers?"

Bexli nodded, her lithe frame and lavender hair transforming into a hulking beast covered in matted fur, with only the slightest hint of purple at the tips. Pog gave a gruff bark and became a green lizard the size of a human, with short legs that scampered across the floor. Both creatures hurried off toward the noise of the enemy bounty hunters boarding their ship.

Danica turned back to the steel door and punched in a code. The door slid open with a groan, revealing a petite figure with short, chocolate-brown hair sitting on the edge of a cot in the sparse room.

"Doctor Dryden," Danica said, her breath ragged. "Some pretty nasty bounty hunters are coming on board to take you. I can promise you they won't be as humane as we've been, but I have a plan that could save us both."

The woman on the cot blinked her wide, blue eyes a few times before answering. "Call me Max."

To be continued . . .

Want to read BOUNTY, book 1 in the Barbarians of the Sand Planet series? Click HERE to keep reading!

ALSO BY TANA STONE

The Tribute Brides of the Drexian Warriors Series:

TAMED (also available in AUDIO)

SEIZED (also available in AUDIO)

EXPOSED (also available in AUDIO)

RANSOMED (also available in AUDIO)

FORBIDDEN (also available in AUDIO)

BOUND (also available in AUDIO)

JINGLED (A Holiday Novella) (also in AUDIO)

CRAVED (also available in AUDIO)

STOLEN (also available in AUDIO)

SCARRED (also available in AUDIO)

ALIEN & MONSTER ONE-SHOTS:

ROGUE (also available in AUDIO)

VIXIN: STRANDED WITH AN ALIEN

SLIPPERY WHEN YETI

CHRISTMAS WITH AN ALIEN

YOOL

Raider Warlords of the Vandar Series:

POSSESSED (also available in AUDIO)

PLUNDERED (also available in AUDIO)

PILLAGED (also available in AUDIO)

PURSUED (also available in AUDIO)

PUNISHED (also available on AUDIO)

PROVOKED (also available in AUDIO)

PRODIGAL (also available in AUDIO)

PRISONER

PROTECTOR

PRINCE

The Barbarians of the Sand Planet Series:

BOUNTY (also available in AUDIO)

CAPTIVE (also available in AUDIO)

TORMENT (also available on AUDIO)

TRIBUTE (also available as AUDIO)

SAVAGE (also available in AUDIO)

CLAIM (also available on AUDIO)

CHERISH: A Holiday Baby Short (also available on AUDIO)

PRIZE (also available on AUDIO)

SECRET

RESCUE (appearing first in PETS IN SPACE #8)

Inferno Force of the Drexian Warriors:

IGNITE (also available on AUDIO)

SCORCH (also available on AUDIO)

BURN (also available on AUDIO)

BLAZE (also available on AUDIO)

FLAME (also available on AUDIO)

COMBUST

THE SKY CLAN OF THE TAORI:

SUBMIT (also available in AUDIO)

STALK (also available on AUDIO)

SEDUCE (also available on AUDIO)

SUBDUE

STORM

All the TANA STONE books available as audiobooks!

INFERNO FORCE OF THE DREXIAN WARRIORS:

IGNITE on AUDIBLE

SCORCH on AUDIBLE

BURN on AUDIBLE

BLAZE on AUDIBLE

FLAME on AUDIBLE

RAIDER WARLORDS OF THE VANDAR:

POSSESSED on AUDIBLE

PLUNDERED on AUDIBLE

PILLAGED on AUDIBLE

PURSUED on AUDIBLE

PUNISHED on AUDIBLE

PROVOKED on AUDIBLE

BARBARIANS OF THE SAND PLANET

BOUNTY on AUDIBLE

CAPTIVE on AUDIBLE

TORMENT on AUDIBLE

TRIBUTE on AUDIBLE

SAVAGE on AUDIBLE

CLAIM on AUDIBLE

CHERISH on AUDIBLE

TRIBUTE BRIDES OF THE DREXIAN WARRIORS

TAMED on AUDIBLE

SEIZED on AUDIBLE

EXPOSED on AUDIBLE

RANSOMED on AUDIBLE

FORBIDDEN on AUDIBLE

BOUND on AUDIBLE

JINGLED on AUDIBLE

CRAVED on AUDIBLE

STOLEN on AUDIBLE

SCARRED on AUDIBLE

SKY CLAN OF THE TAORI

SUBMIT on AUDIBLE

STALK on AUDIBLE

SEDUCE on AUDIBLE

About the Author

Tana Stone is USA Today bestselling sci-fi romance author who loves sexy aliens and independent heroines. Her favorite superhero is Thor (with Aquaman a close second because, well, Jason Momoa), her favorite dessert is key lime pie (okay, fine, *all* pie), and she loves Star Wars and Star Trek equally. She still laments the loss of *Firefly*.

She has one husband, two teenagers, and two neurotic cats. She sometimes wishes she could teleport to a holographic space station like the one in her tribute brides series (or maybe vacation at the oasis with the sand planet barbarians). :-)

She loves hearing from readers! Email her any questions or comments at tana@tanastone.com.

Want to join her VIP Readers list and be the first to know about contests and giveaways? Click here: BookHip.com/CRJHNH

Want to hang out with Tana in her private Facebook group? Join on all the fun at: https://www.facebook.com/groups/tanastonestributes/

ACKNOWLEDGMENTS

Thank you, thank you, thank you to ALL the readers who read my first book, TAMED! Thank you for the reviews and the emails. You have made a new sci-fi romance author very happy!

Special shout-outs to Tanya Saari for her insightful editing, Croco Designs for the fabulous covers, my family for their unending patience, and to all the other SFR authors who have been so supportive and kind. This is such a great genre, in large part because the authors are so cool and the readers are so awesome.

My biggest thanks, as always, is to you, the reader, for reading my books. Writers would be nowhere without readers, so thank you!

Cover Design by Croco Designs

Editing by Tanya Saari

Printed in Great Britain
by Amazon